N.D. 47

A Novel of the New Dispensation

RACHEL WINTERS

Copyright © 2016 Rachel Winters

This book, or parts thereof, may not be reproduced in any form without permission. For information address parasigil66@gmail.com.

Published by: Parasigil Press, The Villages, Florida

ISBN: 978-0-9983437-1-6 / 0-9983437-1-4

Library of Congress Catalog Card Number: 2016918996

First Paperback Edition

For Michael, always, and thank you, Diane Gaffoglio, for your help in bringing this project to life.

When a planet-wide plague left the decimated population in chaos and anarchy, an international nongovernmental aid organization had provided assistance to the stunned survivors. Seeing the need for strong leadership, the directors of the organization named themselves the Conclave of Elders and established the New Dispensation. Ruling as benevolent autocrats, they established a one-world government, banning divisive influences including religion, nationalism, and family solidarity.

By N.D. 47, troubling counterforces were beginning to emerge, challenging the Conclave's total control.

1

"I'm going to meditate now, on the roof." Ana's words were slightly slurred; she had been working for sixteen hours straight. Colt nodded but did not turn around. He was doing dishes and could see her stick figure in baggy jeans and an oversize thermal undershirt in the piece of broken mirror propped on the shelf over the sink. Behind her he could see practically the entire apartment, which was long and narrow. Ana paused by the door. "Be careful crawling around in the dark," he said, watching her face in the mirror over the sink. "Did you have something to eat?"

"Donuts." She ran bony fingers through her short hair, then rubbed her eyes. To Colt, her hair looked dirty. "You would feel better after a shower," he said. She ignored him.

"I picked up some soup. I'll heat it and leave it on the stove. Warm it up when you come down. Not too hot, okay?" he said. She stood, hesitating, with her hand on the door.

"Is it all right if I use the office for my katas? If you're done in there."

Colt didn't expect her to answer, rather expected to hear the door close, but instead she said, "Of course. Are you going out afterward? To play?"

"After I finish my practice." He watched in the mirror as the door closed.

Teegan and Jordi, their roommates, would be home soon, when their shifts ended at the bars in the nearby entertainment district. He still had time to practice without interruption before he went out for the night. Practice and one other thing. He had to call Linnet soon; he worried about her. She was not happy working for Sparrow, and she missed living in the countryside.

On the roof, Ana would be clearing her mind of everything, of thoughts of the project, she said, and, he knew, or feared, of thoughts of him. She was not happy with his gaming. He was afraid one of these nights she would clear him right out of her mind, and her life, permanently. Colt finished the dishes and dried them thoroughly.

Ana forced herself to walk up the ten flights to the roof, the effort helping clear her mind of the project she was working on. Focusing intently for hours was exhausting but the professor's theory that a fatigued brain could be more imaginative and creative led them to work to the limits of sanity, almost to the stage of hallucinating. Lately, however, she had less trouble obsessing over her work because she had begun to be suspicious of Colt. Recently Teegan had made a couple of comments that bothered her, innocent comments about seeing Colt at places he did not mention to Ana. Teegan and Jordi made the rounds of the clubs. They knew everyone and heard everything.

The roof was many stories above the street and slightly higher than the surrounding buildings, giving it an open, spacious feeling rare in the city. Access to the roof was forbidden by the management, but none of the tenants had seen service personnel up there. Nevertheless Ana had constructed a hidden aerie on the top of the shack at the top of the stairwell accessible by an assortment of old boxes and a large garbage can. At this highest point on the roof, she felt especially clearheaded and better able to modulate her breathing. When she finished meditating, Colt would be out and she could grab a few hours of sleep. The project was at a crucial point; regardless of the professor's cockeyed theory that exhaustion released mental creativity, she needed to be fresh.

Colt was finishing his practice when Teegan and Jordi got home from work. Still in his jock strap—he was still too sweaty to dress—he went into the kitchen where Teegan was gazing into the refrigerator and Jordi had just poured himself a vodka. They were a handsome couple, almost like twins, with matching ash blonde hair, dressed alike in standard waiter garb, black pants and shirts. Jordi's shirt had the club logo on the pocket, *psychovator*, a short form of the bar's name, the Psychedelic Elevator, which demonstrated that the club was edgy and fun since certain logos could be construed by the authorities as unsanctioned personal adornment.

To Colt, both seemed unusually emotional. Jordi was somber; Teegan excited.

"Arlo is in town," Jordi said without preamble and downed the entire drink. "Leland saw him in the Subs."

The news accounted for their somber mood. In this context, the Subs referred to the vast network of tunnels and caverns under the bedrock of the city. Many abandoned subway tunnels crisscrossed the Subs; only a few were used by the handful of remaining trains. Untold numbers of citizens lived there, out of view of the city authorities.

"Of course, he would be in the Subs," Teegan said dismissively. "There is a huge bounty for him upside."

"He was supposed to stay away from the city." Jordi poured himself another drink and finished half in one swallow.

"He was supposed to have fled to the countryside; to stay in the city would be suicide." Colt reached past Teegan and grabbed a bottle of sport drink. She made a face at his sweaty shoulder, then licked it. It was no secret, that although in a formal, sanctioned relationship with Jordi, Teegan claimed to favor polyamory and frequently mentioned establishing a group marriage among the four of them.

"Yeah, well, fortunately he didn't get caught by the authorities." Teegan sat at the rickety table and opened a takeout carton. She began eating cold noodles with thin plastic Japanese-style chopsticks. The chopsticks were covered with flattened flower-shaped extrusions that captured food bits in a particularly disgusting way. Jordi thought they resembled antique banana needles. Teegan waved the banana needles at the room. "The question is why did he return."

"He missed his friends," Jordi said, pouring

another drink.

"He has friends everywhere." Teegan shook her head. "He's a legend. He doesn't need to be here in the city, where he's in danger."

"Maybe the authorities forgot about him." Jordi didn't sound convinced.

Colt crumpled the plastic drink bottle and tossed it in the bin. "I haven't forgot about him. For me he's a bad dream that I can't wake up from."

"Anyway, regarding why he came back. They say he came back to see Ana." Teegan pulled out her comm. "I think I'll make a couple of calls, see what I can find out." She put the comm by the takeout container and punched on it with a dirty chopstick while her husband made a disgusted face at her. "Just remember they can track you with that thing. If you mention Arlo and it pops up in their system, they will be at the door in minutes." Teegan made a face at him but quit poking the comm.

"Is Ana still working?" Jordi nodded in the direction of the office.

"Meditating on the roof."

"Are you going to tell her about Arlo?" Teegan finished the noodles and tossed her chopsticks in the trash.

"She's busy with her project. She says they are coming to closure. I don't want to bother her."

"Arlo will want to see her," Teegan warned.

Colt shrugged. "I've got to go. I've got a game tonight." He turned and hurried toward the back of the apartment.

Jordi turned to Teegan and pulled her to her feet. He could smell garlic and sesame. "You going out again?" he asked.

"Yes. Are you?" She gave him a long salty kiss on the lips.

"Let's change clothes and go to Sandy's, see if we can find out what's going on."

Colt waited until Teegan and Jordi left, then tried to reach Linnet, but she was not answering. She was probably working tonight, although she had told him she would be free. She also said she was afraid of the streets, especially at night, but she seemed to go out frequently. Briefly he thought about going by the apartment, checking to see if she was okay. He worried that she would get into an inappropriate relationship. She was so new to the city, so vulnerable.

Before Ana was accepted into Professor Elvistine's institute, they would have been out on the streets partying with Teegan and Jordi. That was also before he had begun gaming every night, before he had dropped out of his usual circles. Despite knowing that the current situation was as much his fault as Ana's— more his fault probably—since he had almost fallen for Linnet, since he couldn't seem to quit gaming, Colt hoped he and Ana had a future. He just couldn't see it.

Colt dressed quickly in old clothes from the scruffy sections of resale shops, no actual holes but worn denim, too big, and soft faded flannel shirts. The work boots had steel toes and high tops that hid a small handgun and knife. Carrying cash tokens was chancy, but the people he played with did not want anything traceable. Not that using cash tokens was completely safe anymore. Some gamblers, those who played for higher stakes, preferred only old money, real cash, completely untraceable. If he could get his hands on some old money, he would be in a position to get into bigger games.

He walked down the sixteen flights of stairs to the street and left the apartment building through the delivery door, then drifted through the alley to exit onto a main street two blocks away. Still a little early for the game, he stopped at the all-night macrobiotic buffet for a leisurely snack of buckwheat noodles and ginger, then stopped at the mini-mart where Singh handed him an empty tin, purporting to be illegal, smokeless tobacco, with the address of tonight's game drawn in marker on the bottom.

Up to that point, he had avoided thinking about the return of Arlo from wherever he had run to when the trouble exploded. Colt knew he could easily find Arlo because, like Arlo, he knew how to navigate the Subs. He turned over in his mind whether it might be better for him and Ana to avoid Arlo as much as possible. Sometime back, lots of people had been looking for Arlo and probably still were, people who wanted Arlo to go away permanently with extreme prejudice. Colt smiled inwardly at the old expression but felt the pain of separation from his friend. Separation from Arlo, separation from Ana. It was all too much.

Then he was at the address written on the tobacco tin, a discreet sign indicating it was a halfway house for graduates of the re-education facilities. A little flip-down shingle read "full up." Colt had played here before. It was always full up. As he put two cash tokens in the tin and slipped it through the mail slot, his heart began to beat faster and he broke a slight sweat in anticipation of the next few hours. Teegan said it was Ana's fault that he had fallen back into gaming; Colt knew better.

Teegan and Jordi held hands as the elevator trundled slowly to the ground floor. The building was old, even grand once upon a time, and the elevator was original. Jordi pushed Teegan against the blue mirror and began some heavy petting, which made her giggle. They had changed into clothing exactly like their work attire sans the pocket logos. Teegan had fluffed out her long hair while Jordi had pulled his into a low ponytail and donned several heavy rings on each hand.

Outside the building, they headed to a side street and hailed a gypsy cab, the driver high on something, surly and unobservant. Everyone in the city cultivated paranoia. The driver dropped them two blocks from Sandy's, a seedy bar in a neighborhood full of seedy bars. Like most of them, Sandy's facade was narrow, half the width of a regular building, with a front window painted black. Inside the bar was deep, at least a block long, and packed with people. The bouncer knew them, waved them through, and they headed over to lean on a wall. The sound system was astoundingly loud; citizens screamed at each other, trying to talk. If you had real business to discuss, you went to the foyer outside the bathrooms or into the bathrooms themselves. While they waited for an opening at the bar, they scanned the crowd looking for anything or anyone out of place. The bartender, middle-aged with a still toned body-builder physique, was shirtless under rainbow suspenders sporting a name tag with a picture of a strange animal and the legend "Hi, my name is Timmy." It wasn't. He made eye contact with Teegan, cocked his head toward the other end of the bar, which was marginally quieter. When Teegan had worked her way through the packed crowd, he lifted the hatch and pulled her behind the bar. They were old friends, fellow bar workers.

"You look worried, Leland," Teegan said, brushing his cheek with the back of her hand. Leland usually extruded a Zen-like professional bartender calm; tonight he seemed agitated. He pulled her close and whispered, "Arlo sent a message. He wants to see Ana. Right away."

Teegan put her arms around him—she loved the feeling of his huge muscles—and whispered back. "Where is he? Did he come in here?"

"He was behind me on the subway train, like a ghost. You know Arlo. Said Ana was in danger, he had to see her."

"Colt won't like it."

"I know," Leland whispered. "I just delivered the message. I've got to get back to work." He pulled her close, in a real hug. "Be careful."

He lifted the flap and let her out. Once on the other side of the bar, he handed her two large vodkas, waving away the cash tokens. Using a more normal voice, he leaned over and said. "Like I said, be careful. There are at least four diggers in here tonight."

Diggers was the new slang for informants, freelance spies. They were paid for reporting unsanctioned behavior to the city authorities. Several people nearby, hearing his words, looked around nervously.

Up front, street light shone through a big scratch in the black-painted window. She could see Jordi listening to another patron, and from her husband's posture, she surmised that he was trying to get rid of the person, who was making the kind of motions with his non-drink hand that left Teegan thinking he was selling something. As she got closer, she recognized the kid as Pelham, a friend from college, who had gone into the army after graduation. Teegan had always like him in a dismissive way—not someone you took seriously, but fun. Although their age, people always thought of Pelham as a kid. He had the slight build and inherent awkwardness of a teenager. In the old days, Jordi and Pelham had been tight. But tonight she could see Jordi trying to get rid of him.

Teegan handed Jordi his vodka. "Hi, Pel, I thought you were in the army," she yelled in his ear.

He looked nervously at the people crowding around them, all apparently oblivious, all carrying on their own screaming conversations.

"Yeah, well, I'm not now."

He put his arms around both their shoulders, pulled their heads toward him. He looked pretty much like he always had with some toughening around the eyes and a bit more swagger. "Let's go out back and talk. I need a smoke."

Teegan glanced at Jordi. Smoking was illegal everywhere, especially in the city. Being seen with a smoker could cause problems. Being a smoker was a ticket to re-education camp. Jordi took another look around. "You go ahead," he said to Pelham, "Teegan and I will go out the front and come around through the alley."

As they strolled outside, Teegan told him what Leland, the bartender, had said about the diggers.

"I know. I spotted two of them," Jordi said.

"Leland puts extra cherries in their free drinks."

Teegan made a skeptical face. "Does that work? Don't they notice?"

Jordi shrugged, "Sometimes. If they were smart, they wouldn't be diggers."

In the middle of the night, the street was still busy with dedicated partiers. They walked down the alley, which was also busy with people conducting various kinds of business. Jordi and Teegan ignored them, as walking slowly toward the back of the bar, they caught the smell of smoke, followed it to Pelham behind a dumpster.

"I don't have much time," he said. "I don't want to be seen with you, get you in trouble." He took a long drag on his cigarette. "When I was in the army, I was assigned to a squad guarding a re-education camp. I got to know some of the diggers who came through to pick up their money."

"Some of those bastards even believe the stories," Pelham said bitterly, although which stories he was referencing was unclear to Jordi, or which bastards.

Stubbing out the cigarette, he sprayed himself, Teegan, and Jordi from a small can. "Helps with the smell," he explained. "Anyhow, I'm out of the army," he paused, "early, and I came to the city to get away from all the believers. Been spending most of my time in the Subs. Got a friend who is showing me around." He smiled briefly, and Teegan seemed to remember that in college he liked boys better than girls. "There's a lot of gossip down there and a lot more diggers than usual snooping around. Not too many in the Subs, of course, or they would be dead diggers." His smile was thin and unpleasant. "Something is happening. They are looking for someone named Arlo, and one of them mentioned a woman named Ana. I remembered an Ana from college, a friend of your roommate Colt. When I saw you in Sandy's tonight, I thought I would pass the word along. If you are still in touch with Colt and Ana, I suggest you tell them to take a long trip."

He pulled a flask out of his pocket and took a pull, held it out to Teegan and Jordi, who both declined, then recapped it.

"You guys are looking good." He gave them both brief hugs, lingering a little with Jordi, then hurried out of the alley.

They heard a blast of music as the back door of the bar opened and closed, then footsteps coming down the alley. Jordi pulled Teegan into a passionate embrace and kissed her, holding the kiss and looking over her shoulder.

"Oh," a voice said. "I thought I smelled smoke." A kid with hair like moldy hay stood in the alley, holding a half glass of liquor with three cherries.

"Want to get beat up?" Jordi flexed his fingers so his rings caught the light.

"No, no, I'm just being a good citizen." The kid backed up quickly, turned.

"He may have been following Pel, and if so, he may follow us," Jordi said. "These guys are opportunistic scum. He may be suspicious. We've got to get rid of him so we can go back to the apartment to warn Ana and Colt. Maybe we'll take a cab. Harder to follow."

They went back inside the bar to have a drink and mull over next steps. Teegan took the opportunity to have a pee which, as usual, took far longer than it needed to because she futzed with her hair and chatted with the bathroom attendant.

Finally when the bar was ready to close, they reluctantly left, looking gingerly around the now almost empty streets. While Jordi stood by the curb waiting for a cab, Teegan wandered over to the mouth of the alley and in a panicky voice called Jordi.

Being followed home by the digger was no longer a problem. When Teegan and Jordi reached the mouth of the alley, they found his body. A thin white chopstick with flower extrusions protruded from his throat. Blood stained his shirt front and puddled on the alley pavement.

Jordi quickly stood up and pulled Teegan into the bar. The crowd was practically gone, and they could get Leland's full attention. He leaned over the bar and Jordi said, "Two vodkas for the road, and there's a body in your alley."

Leland looked offended. "Who is it this time?"

"A digger, don't know his name, blond kid. He was snooping around in back." Teegan was rattled, but Jordi was maintaining a calm front.

"He's no loss then. The authorities will take care of him." Leland looked at Teegan, concerned. "You okay?"

She nodded and sucked down half her drink.

"As far as you know, we've been inside the bar all night," Jordi said.

"As far as I know. As far as I know." Leland went to wait on another "last" customer, and Jordi led Teegan over to an empty table.

"Finish that," he said. "We better get out of here. At least we don't have to worry about the digger following us."

"Do you think Pel did that?" Teegan looked toward the front of the bar.

"Don't know, don't want to know. Maybe. Pel was always kind of volatile. That's why he wanted to go in the army. He thought he might enjoy combat."

"We don't have combat anymore," Teegan said.

"And Pel's not in the army anymore. He retired," Jordi paused, mimicking Pel, "early."

Teegan ran her fingers through her curly hair so it stuck out as if electrified. "I personally hope never to see Pelham what's-his-name ever again."

"Marx, Pelham Marx," Jordi laughed. "May he never darken our door." He tossed off the last of the vodka.

As with much that passes in the human experience, this was so much wishful thinking.

2

While Colt was worrying about Linnet, Linnet was contemplating the mystery that, as she saw it, her life had become. She wondered how she had found herself living in a place she hated – against her expectations, she hated the city – doing work she hated with the people she could not understand. Maybe she should have headed south to one of the big cities down there rather than settling for the city that was closest to her home.

The community where she was born and reared, named Heartsease Commune, was located in a remote, still fertile, valley. It was dedicated to farming and self-sufficiency in preparation for the End Times. Although the Conclave of Elders had saved the world's citizens from complete destruction by the plague, the patriarchs at Heartsease taught that worldwide destruction was imminent for all except those living in Heartsease and similar communities who would be preserved by their pure lifestyle and hard work.

To maintain the pure lifestyle, the community maintained strict guidelines prepared for them personally by members of the Conclave and disseminated by the patriarchs, those very special people tasked with leading the community and who were permitted direct communication with the Conclave. No one questioned the guidelines, and no ever left the community. Outside the valley, they knew, the world was fearsome, lawless, and exquisitely dangerous.

From early in her life, Linnet had wanted to leave, to see the chaos in the outer world so vividly described by the patriarchs. Their descriptions sounded more exciting than fearful to her childish ears. In school, which all children attended for a few years before assuming their appointed roles, she thought she could see what the other children missed, that the teachers were scaring themselves with their stories.

Linnet thought of her childhood as boring. She learned early to keep her questions to herself. She was good in school, but no one cared. Then, when she reached puberty, school ended. She was examined and found to be a breeder. An announcement was made in the morning assembly that she was available for a sanctioned relationship. Oren, a big, slow, stupid boy who, as a son of one of the patriarchs, had been allowed to personally pick his own sanctioned partner, immediately claimed Linnet.

Sanctioned relationships were only available to girls who were capable of providing children to the community and being in such a relationship gave the couple benefits not available to other residents. They were allowed to share a private cottage, and, when the girl conceived, she was relieved of many of the communal chores. Most young women enjoyed the benefits of the sanctioned relationship and were envied by their infertile friends. Linnet was miserable. She hated sex and feared pregnancy. Oren was surprised at her attitude. He had been taught that the epitome of a woman's life was having children because children were essential to the continuation of Heartsease. The members lived for continuation of Heartsease. Heartsease was everything.

Unintentionally he gave her clues how to escape. It had never occurred to her how supplies needed by the community arrived from the outer world. Like others who had been born there, she accepted that they were gifts from the C.E. The community was largely self-sufficient but woven cloth and building materials, for example, appeared when they were needed.

Through conversations with her new husband, she learned that the patriarchs had lucrative financial affairs outside the community, that the crops the community raised were sold, not stored for the End Times in the big storehouses as they were told. During daylong assemblies, behind the backs of the members, trucks would come in to pick up the crops and move them for sale outside the valley. Once she knew about the trucks, she was able to escape to the city.

Unexpectedly, she had become fond of Oren and hoped that he was not punished too severely for her escape. Someone was always punished when the patriarchs discovered a runaway. Stern warnings would be delivered about the dangers outside, how leaving was almost certain death or worse. And it was true. No one who left ever returned.

Linnet looked around the little room and contemplated her future. She stared at herself in the mirror, a novelty to her, as they were strictly forbidden at home, and rare outside, then braided her waist-length hair into a tight pigtail that could be wound up under a cap. Tonight she had to go into the Subs, a trip she dreaded. She was repelled by the dark souls she met in the tunnels, the eternal pale lamplight, the appointment she had to keep.

The apartment Teegan and Jordi shared with Ana and Colt was long and narrow, carved out of two older apartments in an ancient building. Aside from the cheap rent, the main advantage of the situation was two bathrooms with plumbing that usually worked. Each couple had a large room of their own and shared the kitchen and central common space. When Teegan and Jordi returned from Sandy's, they found Ana asleep on the sofa.

She had obviously been unable to make it to her bedroom.

"Leave her where she is," Teegan stretched. "She'll wake up to take a pee and crawl back to her room."

"Speaking of taking a pee, you were in the bathroom a long time tonight." Jordi untied his ponytail and shook it out.

"Was I?" She was exquisitely disinterested. "I was talking to Norma, the new bathroom girl. She's from down south, some place with a lot of water, squatting with a group of girls in one of those abandoned buildings downtown. She says it's not too bad."

"If you don't need plumbing or running water." Jordi was poking through the garbage can. He couldn't find the chopsticks he distinctly remembered seeing Teegan throw away earlier in the evening.

"Better than where she came from, I'll bet." Teegan gestured toward the garbage can. "You lose something, Baby?"

"What? No." Now he pretended disinterest. "I thought I smelled something funny."

"Then take it downstairs and throw it on the curb with the rest of the garbage."

"Maybe later," Jordi said. "What do you think happened to the digger?"

"He died. It happens a lot to diggers. They make a lot of enemies. Bastards." Teegan made a strange ethnic gesture that Jordi was sure he had not seen before, a kind of cursing gesture, he imagined. He envisioned an old woman squatting with other old witches by a campfire making that gesture. Teegan straightened up, visibly getting control of herself. Her fear of diggers was extreme.

"Bedtime, Baby. You coming?" Teegan asked.

"You go ahead." Then adding, "I wish I still smoked."

"Too dangerous, you know that. Snort something." She indicated a pile of glassy envelopes and bottles on top of the refrigerator.

"No. Sometimes I just miss real tobacco."

Jordi was exhausted after working a full shift and spending hours at Sandy's, but he didn't think he could sleep. He could not get the picture of the digger's neck with the thin plastic chopstick sticking out, the blood, the sight of death. He wished he couldn't begin to contemplate the possibility that Teegan had killed the guy. Briefly Jordi wished he knew the digger's name. It seemed hard to be dead and nameless, even though, Jordi reminded himself, the digger presented a threat to Teegan and himself. Anyone could be found doing something that violated the laws of the New Dispensation. Smoking seemed to be one of their major shibboleths, but they were also opposed to tattoos, jewelry, paper books, a long list of personal adornment items including certain scarves, tee shirts, beards. A determined digger could always find something to snitch on.

Leland's message from Arlo had rattled both of them because they had understood that Arlo was at the top of not just the city authorities' wanted list but the C.E.'s list. Just being seen by the wrong person talking with Arlo could result in an immediate trip to a re-education facility, probably one of those from which no one returned.

At one time, Arlo had been deeply in love with Ana.

Jordi sprawled in a chair and watched Ana sleep. He wondered what Ana really felt for Arlo. She would say she was angry with him, that she was glad he was gone. In the old days, before she hooked up with Colt, she had been close to Arlo. All the suitemates had been close. He could not remember anything remarkable about Ana and Arlo. He and Teegan had been surprised when she hooked up with Colt but, Jordi thought sadly, who knew about love. While you were young, you wanted to be in love; when you got older, you regarded it as an unfortunate accident.

Teegan was the only girl Jordi had loved and not only because she was willing to have regular sex with him. His parents were from the professional classes. His father was a professor of engineering, his mother the director of nursing at a large clinic in the city.

Both had been devoted to their two children, trying to ensure they would have professions when they finished school. Unlike most parents who sent their children to sanctioned schools in the countryside, they kept their children at home where they could supervise their upbringing and education. They made sure Jordi and his older sister had tutoring to augment the regular electronic education offered by the public schools and subtly bribed the kids' way into college. It had put him at a disadvantage over those who went to boarding schools in the countryside because he was sheltered. For example, he didn't know any girls except his sister and her friends, who alternated between ridiculing and ignoring him.

His best friend growing up was probably the family's housekeeper and nanny Roxa Baer, who had time to do caregiving while his parents worked. Especially after his sister left home, Jordi had her full attention. Now he remembered those few years as ones of happy contentment although at the time he was busy with school, tutoring, and mandatory physical education. Like many country people, Roxa Baer had a deep distrust, even deeper than his parents' more rational caution, of the government and all authority, distrust that rubbed off on Jordi.

Then in college, his first time away from home, he ended up in a dorm suite with Teegan, Colt, Ana, Arlo, and another girl named Daphne, inevitably called Daffy. During a brief foray into cartooning, Jordi has drawn them all: Teegan the femme fatale; Colt the rescuer; Ana the brainiac; Arlo the hothead; and Daffy the clueless rich girl. He couldn't come up with a cartoon identity for himself. His personality had seemed to him to be vague, anomalous. Once he got away from home and the constant external pressure to get into college, he found that, as Arlo had said, he lacked the ambition gene. Arlo had added, darkly, "And that's going to save your sanity and maybe your life some day." As with so many of Arlo's gnomic statements, Jordi had no idea what he was talking about.

Still growing up without close friends, boys or girls, Jordi found himself, with Colt and Arlo, spending all night discussing forbidden topics, speculating about the C.E.'s various peculiar laws, even reading old books Arlo found exploring empty campus buildings.

They talked about their plans. Jordi's professional family had identified his goal: obtaining a degree, followed by work for a big industrial firm. He enrolled in engineering classes but, despite the endless tutoring, was weak in math. Ana helped with that.

Ana herself came from a family of academics, all either mathematicians or musicians. She had been in schools for gifted children from the time she was four, and everyone knew she would do something extraordinary.

Colt, on the other hand, was a mediocre student. Because he was physically attractive, blond with grey eyes and long dark lashes, and intensely shy, he hid behind Ana and Teegan. His military family intended him to join the army when he graduated. An accomplished athlete, a champion lacrosse star in secondary school, and a cage fighter in college, he would have no problem achieving their goal. Although there was no combat or war under the N.D., the military was needed for management in backward regions that resisted the benevolent direction of the Conclave of Elders. Professional athletic activities had been banned in the public sector; the C.E. mandated that all professional athletes would be in the military.

Only Arlo had no stated goal. His parents were counselors who helped citizens formulate correct thoughts about issues that might bother them, *i.e.*, professional re-educators. According to Arlo, they were both personally dysfunctional; his father a dreamer and his mother a latent hedonist. Like Jordi, Arlo had an alternative parent figure, his father's sister, who lived with them and cared for Arlo and Arlo's sister. In college, Arlo was enrolled in courses in Social Arts and had eventually been accepted into the prestigious Marketing and Propaganda Program.

Jordi remembered going with Arlo for some holiday or other to visit his parents in their beautiful home in a small coastal village. The adults were welcoming, but Jordi felt their intense interest and attention focused on him, asking his opinions, drawing him out, something no one had done before. Their regard was kindly, but he felt an undercurrent of something he could not identify, a certain ruthlessness, perhaps, that he read as a threat. He lacked the experience and sophistication to analyze the uncertainty their close intent raised in his mind, and it drove him to withdraw from them. On the trip back to school, Arlo asked him his opinion of "the parents" and Jordi tried to express his discomfort. Arlo had laughed and said something like, "You have to love them. They'll eat your soul." Arlo was always using outré expressions and causing Jordi to scan his surroundings to see if anyone was listening.

It was sometime after that trip that Jordi started

spending more time with the girls, especially Ana and Teegan. Colt spent most of his spare time in the dojo or on the lacrosse field—fitness was required for an army career—and Arlo had joined a series of informal groups that included speculation and intellectual explorations that Jordi felt verged on the illegal.

Besides Arlo's increasingly eccentric interests, Jordi was relying more and more on Ana for help with his classes. While exceptionally strong with visual relationships—he could draw what he saw perfectly to scale—he lacked the vision and analytic creativity to formulate the invisible relationships that are essential for success as a mathematician.

However, socializing with Ana was almost impossible. Her interpersonal skills were marginal, everything you said to her was taken personally. She could not be teased and had no understanding of jokes. Jordi didn't think she understood that other people were as human as she was. Or maybe she didn't consider herself human but a kind of mammal machine. He had much preferred Teegan and Daffy as buddies, but Daffy grew increasingly involved with her work, leaving him with Teegan. Daffy had been accepted into the Applied Arts program that would allow her to graduate as a sanctioned artist. The work was intensive, and all her time was devoted to working or sleeping. That left Teegan, who spent most of her downtime drinking. Jordi found himself developing a taste for vodka.

Daffy eventually left their suite and moved in with a boyfriend from the Social Arts program she met through Arlo. Left together, Teegan and Jordi had been a couple ever since and in a sanctioned relationship for two years.

In the bedroom, Teegan slipped out of her clothes and threw them in the laundry basket. Her and Jordi's bedroom was sparsely furnished with an elderly futon and a bookshelf with pull out baskets for storage. A huge old wardrobe, intricately carved, was the room's only attractive feature, and it would have been sold long before if one of the ornate doors was not broken. Teegan took a towel from the wardrobe and slid her hand behind a piece of loose carving to retrieve a small comm. Hiding the comm in the towel, she went into the bathroom and locked the door.

A chemical shower had been rigged up in a corner of the room and a built-in cabinet dominated another corner. Hot, running water was available in the sink and Teegan turned it on for maximum noise, then pushed some buttons to activate the comm. Watching the message on the tiny screen, her expression reflected disappointment and anger. Shutting off the instrument, she hid it behind some personal items in the cabinet and got ready for bed.

Jordi listened for the familiar nighttime sounds and the closing of the bedroom door before he hauled himself out of the comfortable chair and headed toward their bathroom. Bothering Teegan in the bathroom was not a safe thing to do.

Teegan had grown up in a commune consisting of six sets of parents and innumerable kids. The six families had bought an old motel, each family sleeping in a small bungalow and sharing all other activities. Everyone shared a common kitchen, laundry, and lavatory facilities, and privacy was unknown. Teegan had hated the crowded conditions; when she left home for the university she was delighted to discover that the assigned six-person suite had private water closets.

She had little positive words for her childhood except to say that, although the kids were home-schooled and had no significant tutoring, most of them excelled at the national tests and were able to go to university. Jordi was never clear on the number of kids in the extended family because Teegan only mentioned two who were close to her in age. She rarely mentioned her parents and never talked about siblings. When they were getting serious about their relationship, and after Jordi had invited her to meet his family, she was reluctant to revisit the commune.

At university, Teegan had developed into a professional drinker, never too intoxicated, never acting out, just usually getting quiet and seriously putting away the liquor. She cultivated cool indifference and avoided scenes. Therefore the occasional outburst was memorable, as when an elderly man came into the bar accompanying a very young girl with whom he was obviously having some kind of intimate relationship. Teegan pointed them out to Jordi, bitterly, calling the old man a bastard and threatening to follow the girl into the toilet and warn her that he was using her. Teegan had begun to cry, sending Jordi into impotent shock. She kept saying "just like Crowley, the bastard, the bastard." Then she dried her eyes and said firmly, "But we took care of him. We killed the bastard."

When Jordi later asked her about Crowley, she refused to discuss him, laughing and changing the subject.

Jordi had refused to drop the topic completely.

"But you said you killed him. You didn't mean that, did you?" And Teegan had brushed him off, saying, "If we did, he deserved it." Then laughing again, had said, "It's all old history."

Another time, in a club, a young man approached Teegan. Seeing him, she became visibly upset and tried to ignore him, but he stood between Teegan and Jordi, saying, "Teegan, what a surprise. I lost track of you after you left for the university."

"Hello, Watson," Teegan had said. Her voice indicated to Jordi that she was dangerously pissed. "What are you doing here?" She didn't introduce the two men.

Watson told them he had been recruited for the army rugby team and was spending his last two weeks of civilian life partying in the city. Although not as tall as Jordi, he had the blocky litheness coupled with suppressed hostility that seemed to characterize rugby. He showed a tendency to hang around, asking Teegan questions which she blew off, finally going to the ladies' room to get away. When she left, Watson looked at Jordi, hands in the pockets of his very tight pants. "Teegan didn't introduce us. I'm Watson Fletcher, from the commune. Teegan and I grew up together. You and Teegan a couple?"

"We're in a sanctioned relationship," Jordi said.

"Really," Watson looked surprised. "Teegan in a sanctioned union. Well, good luck, Jordi. How long have you been together?" Jordi told him. Although Watson was obviously ready to move on, he had an exit line. "Really, that long? And you're still alive. I can see you've found ways not to piss her off." He disappeared into the crowd.

When Teegan returned, Jordi had asked her about

Watson but she had refused to say anything. "He's always been a zero, Watson, excessively lame. Everybody knows army athletes are thugs."

"All professional athletes are in the military now," Jordi had said.

"I know. Let's go get a drink."

Watching Ana sleep and listening to the familiar nighttime sounds, Jordi could not wrap his mind around the idea that Teegan could kill someone and especially with a chopstick to the neck, a brutal, efficient move, a move that required being very close to the still-living body of the victim. Wouldn't blood spurt over your hand? Jordi remembered the amount of blood on the digger's neck. Another colder voice in his head reminded him that a door to the alley opened off the back hallway to the toilets. Easy to stab someone in the alley, then pop in and wash the blood off your hands. The attendant might notice but would she care? She was there to keep people from having sex and taking drugs in the toilet, not to monitor blood on murderers' hands.

He looked around the apartment, watching Ana sleep on the couch in the living room, wondering if everything in his life was going to hell. Arlo was back, and Teegan was missing a chopstick.

3

Linnet walked the streets, blending in with the other featureless citizens. After the constant scrutiny in the community, she felt strange and invisible, having no one constantly monitoring her existence. She welcomed the anonymity, of course, now realizing, like all city dwellers, that you were only in danger when someone was watching you. At the moment, she was not paying attention to the streets as she should because she was thinking about Ozzie the Ocelot, a video show about an anthropomorphized version of an extinct wild cat. In the video, Ozzie experienced many unusual adventures, all with a moral, about life in the New Dispensation and the improvements the N.D. had brought to the lives of the world's citizens. Linnet ignored the subtext, having grown up immersed in the messages of the C.E. Only educational videos had been allowed in Heartsease and that strictly monitored. She had never been introduced to the adventures of Ozzie and his friends.

She was worried about Ozzie. He was a tremendously friendly little ocelot, and he had befriended a mangy anteater, another extinct animal Linnet had seen in pictures. But the anteater in the video was clearly leading Ozzie into trouble. Linnet wished she could go back to the times before the animals were extinct, before the greedy, callous people destroyed everything.

Ozzie was so cute, so purple, not like a cat at all. The cats in the city were all ordinary brown and gray. The teachers said the old people used to capture cats and other animals called dogs and keep them in their houses. Linnet was skeptical about this. Sometimes the stories the teachers told about the old people seemed ridiculous. Everyone knew that animals other than valuable stock like goats and cows were riddled with disease. One scratch would leave you sick for weeks, maybe dead.

Lots of people in the Subs, or on the downside, as she was coming to call it, actually touched the animals down there and seemed to be okay but she, Linnet, was not taking chances. The teachers lied about a lot of things, but she could not imagine why they would lie about that.

Colt left the gaming room, having won big. The mixture of exhilaration and sweaty adrenaline overcame for a few minutes the shadow of gnawing depression and fear that had been building for months. Tonight he had won, which accounted for the exhilaration; but having won, he knew he would lose. The gaming gods, Lady Luck, and the laws of chance were unerring. Ana had explained, sometimes even in words he could understand, the futility of trying to beat the cosmic forces of numbers, her gods. He knew she was right, but the feeling of sitting across from other warriors of chance, hearing the hypnotic click of the Mah Jongg tiles, had completely seduced his spirit overwhelming his love for Ana and his dreams of getting back into the army, of making his parents proud. He acknowledged that latter dream, his dream that his parents would someday be proud of him was more in the nature of a fantasy. Maybe, he thought, the knowledge that his parents' pride was almost entirely an illusion made letting go of his army goals easier. He had been happy to leave the army when the opportunity had presented itself. Then he immediately regretted his choice. Recently, against Ana's wishes, he had begun the process of seeking readmission to the military, having quit, in the first place, to be with her.

Even as he hurried through the mostly empty streets, flush with coin tokens and even illegal old paper money, he was forced to acknowledge, through some remaining mote of self respect, that his army goal had never been about making his parents proud. Indeed they were pretty much indifferent to his accomplishments, but you needed to tell the psychologists that you were doing it for your parents or for the Conclave when you were being considered for military service. He had opted for naming his parents and sometimes you come to believe your lies. In reality, he now thought he wanted to go back into the army to face the challenges, to show he had not lost his skills and nerve.

Suddenly Colt realized he was hungry, couldn't remember the last time he had eaten. He had some soup, he thought, when he fixed Ana's meal, but that had been many hours before. No, maybe he had some noodles. He seemed to remember going into a noodle shop. As he paused outside a small all-night diner, he heard footsteps running behind him and reflexively reached for his knife.

"No, no." It was a fellow player he had met at the match, Chandler. "We're heading in the same direction," he said, laughing. Chandler had a happy-go-lucky edge that Colt thought might actually be genuine. He was younger than Colt, living, Colt thought, mostly in the Subs. His waist-long hair was braided, clearly not a sanctioned style, with a little metal ball woven in at the end. Colt knew that such devices could become deadly weapons in the right hands. Did Chandler have the right hands?

"I was just going to stop for some food." Colt said, indicating the little shop.

"You'll have to buy. I lost big," Chandler said.

He had been losing when Colt had played with him earlier, before changing tables. His expertise was difficult to assess. His movements were professional. But his play, Colt questioned his play. Maybe he was just unlucky.

"Didn't get any better?"

"No. Worse, if anything." His companion laughed again.

They went into the bright shop and yelled to wake the waiter, who was dozing in a corner, ordered stir fry tofu and vegetables full of garlic. The waiter found a couple of bottles of beer, which Chandler declined, making a gesture toward his stomach and shaking his hand back and forth. "Not on an empty stomach," he said.

Maybe he wasn't so happy-go-lucky after all.

They ate quickly and silently with thin plastic chopsticks that Jordi would have recognized. Food was never very tasty under the N.D. because, they were told, the greed and wanton waste of the previous generations had destroyed all the animals. Food was fuel, not entertainment.

They replayed the night's action, and Chandler marveled at how Colt had made several hands, seemingly from nothing, how he seemed to block other players. Colt tried to explain how he made choices, but he and Chandler both knew you cannot rationalize these things. Either the tiles come to you and you recognize the patterns or they don't. He had known times when he recognized, too late, a pattern he could have won with. Other times, he had needed only a tile or two from the beginning, and they had never showed up. Colt had given up trying to figure it out.

"Why do you think we do this?" he asked Chandler, uncharacteristically forthright.

Chandler looked surprised. Colt had seemed stolid, uncommunicative, rude, really. He shrugged his shoulders. "What else?" Why was Colt asking these questions? "I don't know. It's all I want to do."

"Don't you recognize me?" He continued. "I was in the Advanced Math Department with your girlfriend Ana."

Colt had not remembered him. Ana never introduced her department friends.

"Ana never talked about the department," Colt said.

"I know. She is pretty focused, just brilliant." Chandler leaned forward, as if imparting a delightful secret. "An amazing ability. We were all blown away by her gifts." He paused, then said, a little too casually, "Is she still working with Elvistine?"

"I believe so," Colt said. "Why?"

"He's kind of a brilliant kook, you know. Some even think he is going in a dangerous direction."

"Dangerous?" This seemed a new concept to Colt. "Elvistine's a theorist." He paused, enlightened. "You mean the protesters. They have it in for anyone doing deep science. I don't understand it myself. Ana says they are stupid."

"Oh, I was not talking about the protesters. They are stupid. I was talking about, you know, the time thing."

There was a silence. Chandler suddenly changed posture and topic, hitting Colt up for a "loan," which Colt gave him, thinking Chandler was wearing a very expensive, very stylish suit, his pigtail with the silver ball swinging gracefully.

"Would you take some old money?" Colt hated to let go of any of the old money, but he wanted to see if Chandler would take it.

"Sure. It actually is worth more than cash tokens downside." Chandler used the in-group slang for the Subs. Before Colt could ask more questions, Chandler was up and out of the little restaurant, flitting away, saying he would pay Colt back at the next game.

Colt knew Chandler would likely not be at the next game; and if he was, he would have forgotten the "loan."

Suddenly exhausted, Colt went home, pausing briefly to call Linnet without getting an answer. He had given her a comm and showed her how to use it, so he was beginning to worry about her. She was unequipped for life in the city, said she hated it. Her boss was good to her, and she had made friends among her fellow workers. Lately, though, she was seldom there, and tonight he didn't have the energy to check on her.

As he walked, he was troubled by his conversation with Chandler and by his own state of mind. Colt consciously tried to live on the surface, necessary for survival as a soldier, martial artist, and gambler. He needed complete focus on the external world, on the behavior, the small revealing movements of the people in his world, without the distraction of thoughts or emotions. Now he found himself questioning his behavior, his relationship with Ana. Why had he extended himself to Chandler, exposing himself?

The morning was well advanced and the sky almost completely light when he reached the apartment. He expected Ana to be at the university, but she was lying on the sofa in the living room staring into space. He brushed the hair off her forehead and kissed her. "Don't," she pushed him away, saying, " You smell of garlic."

"I ran into a guy named Chandler. We had a meal together. He said he knew you from the department."

"Chandler," she said his name in a musing way. "He was a math guy, very bright. I don't know what happened to him. He graduated and disappeared." She gave Colt a sharp look. "I see, he's gambling with you. That's where you ran into him."

Colt threw his backpack on the floor and collapsed into a chair. He was exhausted. "This was the first time I actually talked with him. I've just seen him around, I think. He says he spends most of his time downside."

Ana disapproved of the downside. "He should talk to the professor. We could use someone with his skills on the project." Frowning, "Have you got contact information for him? I should talk to him."

"I'll see what I can do. By the way, Chandler mentioned something interesting about the professor. He said the professor was a gifted kook—I can't remember the exact words—maybe some other kind of kook, and that this project you are working on might be dangerous. He called it "the time thing." What's he talking about? Are you involved in something dangerous?"

Ana made a disgusted face, jumped up, very animated now. "Dangerous! These idiots, these protesters don't know what they are talking about. They are so credulous. They think because the professor set up the protocol for contact between parallel universes, about which everyone was sooooo doubting, that everything he does will have bad effects."

Colt said, "But the parallel protocol didn't really do anything. I thought all that happened was some static noise and a power surge." True, he didn't pay attention to the news videos, but contacting parallel universes had been big news. Elvistine had been famous. Then it died down. The authorities said they were exploring it further, and the story completely dropped out of sight.

Ana frowned. "The protocol had a few more effects than that; not the protocol, of course, but the actual contact. There were some concerns stemming from the exchange of information."

"There was nothing about an exchange of information in the news," Colt said. "I'll bet the old farts were in a tizzy if there was actual information coming from the contact, not just static electricity." He laughed.

"There was a code," Ana said austerely. "Very difficult to understand and then the language problem." She shook her head, but Colt knew her well enough to know she was proud of her accomplishment. " It took me, us, a long time."

"And what was the message from the other side?"

"It was not a message, exactly. It was more a threat. They seemed concerned that we had made contact and that we might be threatening them. They actually seemed to know a lot about us."

"They were not happy that we had found a way to make contact." Colt thought that surprising. To him, it seemed astonishing, even wonderful.

"Not at all. They wanted all transmissions to cease immediately."

"But I take it all transmissions did not cease immediately?"

"Why do you say that?"

"Because it isn't our way. Once we have a new toy, we need to play with it."

"It wasn't that we were unwilling to cease transmissions. We were directed from the very highest levels of the Conclave of Elders to cease transmissions."

"I take it something happened."

"It turns out that the channel cannot be closed, at least by us. We have to monitor it 24 hours a day and guard it from everyone, but it is still open. The other side seems satisfied as long as nothing comes through."

Colt thought briefly that he might be hallucinating. He was tired, and the story Ana was telling him seemed outlandish.

"So is it dangerous?" he asked.

"It might be, if they get angry. A spectrum of sub-sub-atomic energy is coming through that we don't have equipment to measure. Who knows what would happen if organisms came through the channel. Even organisms that are harmless to them might kill us."

"Or vice versa." Colt said, suddenly appreciating the concerns of the other side.

"Well, yes, that is their concern," Ana sounded like she was contemplating a rather unimportant point.

"Is the famous Dr. Elvistine monitoring the channel?"

"Dr. Elvistine is doing other things. The army is monitoring the channel. They have very competent mathematic academicians of their own. Dr. Elvistine has moved on."

"To the time thing." Colt said.

"To the time thing."

"And what is the time thing that Chandler thinks is dangerous?"

"Do you really need to know this?"

Ana's sharp tone irritated Colt, and he said nothing, merely frowned and waited.

She fiddled with her hair, not looking at him. "We, the professor and the team, are doing an academic exercise. We are very close to accomplishing it, too. That's why I have been working so hard." She paused, as if considering how much to tell him.

"It's simple really. We have almost completed a proof that time could not exist."

This announcement was an anticlimax to Colt. He was expecting news about a weapon. The professor was initially famous for discovering a way to power a weapon called the moon-buster because it was powerful enough to destroy the moon. The moon-buster had really made it possible for the New Dispensation to become a reality. He and a fellow researcher at the university named Menard Tillman had together discovered a truly incredible way to create fusion power which could, among other things, instantly dissolve any material object, organic or inorganic. When citizens disappeared, it was usually via a fusion pistol.

A proof that time could not exist was meaningless, like the contents on a box of cereal. Time would still go on even if it did not exist. You ate the cereal even though it was composed of unpronounceable compounds.

"Of course time exists," he found himself saying.

"Laymen always say that," Ana said. "But really there is no proof for it, no scientific proof, only experiential."

"But you always say that proving a negative is impossible."

"I might have been wrong. Besides we are not proving that time doesn't exist, but that it cannot possibly exist."

"What about Einstein?" Colt knew almost nothing about science, but he had heard of Einstein and the idea of relativity.

"Einstein," Ana said, with contempt, "was 95 percent religion. We are about science."

"And why is this proof dangerous? It won't make a difference in anything."

"You know, Colt, people are superstitious. They are afraid this will be like the parallel universes protocol. That it will have unintended consequences."

"What consequences could it have?" Colt thought he could see where this was heading.

"Oh, they are afraid knowledge might affect reality; some people think reality is solely knowledge and not material. They are afraid a proof that time could not exist would abolish time. The sun might fall out of the sky. It might be Armageddon."

"What's Armageddon?" Another new term. With Ana there were always new terms.

"The end of the world," said Ana, "the end of the world."

4

Jordi and Teegan came home just then and ended the conversation between Colt and Ana. The newcomers were avid with news.

Teegan threw herself into a chair, rocking back and forth like a child. Jordi poured himself a drink.

They both talked at once and so confusing was their story that Ana and Colt both thought Pelham had been stabbed.

Colt, who was himself practically vibrating from exhaustion, tried in vain to put a face to the name, but Ana remembered him.

"This is very odd," she said, "two members of the advanced math program turning up in the same day. And now one of them dead." She sounded worried.

"Dead? Who's dead" Teegan said.

"You said this person named Pelham had been murdered," Colt said.

"No, you misunderstood. A digger got murdered. We think Pel might have murdered him. He told us that someone was looking for you and Ana. He said you were in danger, that you should get out of town. It has something to do with Arlo. He's back in the city, hiding downside, and he wants to see Ana."

"I won't see him," Ana said. "It is too dangerous. And besides I am mad at him. He spread stories."

"True stories," Teegan said.

Ana was angry. "They were not his to tell, and he got a lot of people in trouble with them. People who were innocent."

"Leland, the bartender at Sandy's, also said Arlo wanted to see Ana," Jordi said.

"I don't care," Ana said. "I won't see him. I don't know why he wants to see me anyway after what he did."

"He was in love with you," Teegan said.

"Then he had a very poor way of showing it," Ana said.

"They can all go to the stasis chamber for all I care," Colt said. "I'm going to bed."

Arlo Gauss was a small man, prematurely bald, with large, protruding ears, the thin rims of which seemed to turn slightly when he needed to pick up conversations. For a person with his habits and associations, extreme hearing was very useful. At the moment, he was riding in a subway train four seats away from a digger of his acquaintance. This digger, one Cosmo Naftali, was working with Arlo because Arlo had led him to believe that he could show him the hiding place of a person for whom a large bounty had been published. Cosmo had confided to Arlo that digging was not as lucrative as it had been and was becoming more dangerous, hence he was thinking about branching out into bounty hunting. Arlo wondered, if avoiding danger was Cosmo's goal, how turning in to the authorities even more dangerous people than the largely innocuous citizens he usually targeted could be better. Arlo did not inquire too deeply about Cosmos's rationale for upping the stakes jobwise; he had uses for Cosmo.

Arlo had been back in the city for a while now, and he wanted to establish contact with Colt and Ana, especially Ana. He was anxious to see Ana again, to clarify some issues between them. Shortly after he had arrived in the city and bunked with friends in the Subs, he had been made aware via those friends that someone was looking for Ana and Colt, that a large amount of cash had been offered to anyone who could find Ana or Colt or both in an incriminating behavior.

Arlo puzzled with his Subs friends about this rumor. Anyone could easily find Ana. She was at the university, and following her back to the apartment would be easy. Where Ana was, Colt would be. As for finding incriminating behavior, so many things were illegal that anyone on the street could legitimately be accused of four or five illegal things. Eating hot dogs was illegal; wearing shirts that displayed numbers or pictures of certain cartoon characters, wearing vintage leather sandals, having a mustache that exceeded the sanctioned length. Colt was still, Arlo expected, gambling, and gambling was illegal, as was holding old money, which most gamblers did.

The enigma bothering Arlo was that his friends in Grupo Uno were unable to identify the source of the offer. Grupo Uno was one of the largest gangs in the Subs with extensive contacts. Although the population of the Subs was huge and primarily consisted of loners with differing substance abuse and mental problems, runaways, and misfits, numerous formal and informal groups lived there out of sight of the sanctioned world. Arlo's friends in Grupo Uno were well connected within the Subs; their businesses included arranging transportation from the city to other cities without attracting attention, selling scarce legal and even scarcer illegal pharmaceuticals, and various protection schemes. By maintaining a policy of strict neutrality and integrity, they managed to protect themselves and maintain ties throughout the network of Subs. Much of their success came from their close work with the floating population of governments agents, diggers, and provocateurs who labored in both worlds. It was pretty much a sure thing that anyone new to the Subs would come to Grupo's attention quickly and their business identified and evaluated. Those deemed a threat to Grupo or to those under Grupo's protection would be neutralized or disappear permanently. Grupo had a lassiez-faire attitude toward mayhem that did not directly affect themselves, but closely monitored the police, secret or otherwise, who might come into the Subs. Depending on their activities, they might return to upside or they might disappear. The Subs were dangerous.

It was inconceivable that Grupo would not know who was looking for Ana and Colt, yet Arlo believed their denials. Like Arlo, Grupo was mostly composed of Osirans, an illegal religion, but low on the hit list of the C.E. Osirans tended to be honest at least with each other. Yet the rumor about Ana and Colt had recently spread throughout the Subs and, like all rumors, everyone heard it from someone else.

Arlo had been hanging out in a bar on the upside, far from the neighborhood where he might accidentally run into any of his old crowd, when he got in conversation with Cosmo. They had known each other at university. Cosmo had once dated Arlo's friend Pelham. Like Pelham, Cosmo himself had been in the army, but it had not been a good fit. He was not ingratiating enough to get good postings and got tired of finding himself on the perimeters of cities around the world shooting citizens who were trying to escape. When his enlistment ended, he had smuggled himself back to the city where he had friends and settled in as a digger.

The pay was good and kept him in food and drugs and rented a room upside. He was fortunately able to move back and forth freely between the worlds. But diggers tended to get beat up a lot. He was contemplating a change.

Over bourbon, Cosmo discussed his planned transition from digger to bounty hunter, which, as he saw it, he could do once a year and be set for the entire year rather than hustling for small-time transgressors all year long. Arlo was noncommittal. There was a large bounty on himself of which Cosmo seemed unaware. Arlo didn't mention it.

Cosmo then began lamenting the recent increasing craziness in the city and the establishment of the protesters, which discussion itself could get him sent to a re-education camp, and the growing presence of a new group known as the Command, ostensibly the most secret of the secret groups.

Under the New Dispensation, in which each citizen was a potential criminal, the police tended to keep a low profile. The C.E. had their own militia for personal defense, and all police reported to them through an upward chain of bureaucracy. In the N.D., all police were secret police.

Rumors of the Command were recent. Previously the group was almost completely unknown. It was said that they reported directly to the Conclave, to certain individual elders personally. Their mission was to uncover and disarm direct threats to the C.E. and to the New Dispensation itself that the army could not handle. Most citizens both upside and in the Subs who heard about the group were unclear what those threats could be. Were they religious groups who were still fighting or nationalistic cabals? With the abolishment of countries, the C.E. claimed wars were no longer fought.

"I've heard some big battles are being fought in other parts of the globe," Arlo said.

Cosmo agreed that was the case, but said, "They are just uprisings of the unenlightened and are doomed to failure against the army, who were better armed, organized, and fed."

The Command would not care about them. Its focus, such as could be determined, was internal threats to the C.E. Citizens were always trying to kill members of the C.E. when some new law or other disenfranchised them. Trying to kill elders was totally understandable. Most citizens secretly cheered for those who tried, but they were hugely unsuccessful, and the elders' guards routinely stopped them. The Command, on the other hand, had started emerging in urban areas as faceless people whom no one knew but who seemed to know everything. The name itself was apparently given them by outsiders. No one knew what they called themselves. Unlike the authorities who patronized the diggers, the Command was interested in having specific people seriously compromised. Once that was done, the person passing on the information would mysteriously receive large cash and the party of interest would disappear.

The authorities would not investigate the disappearance of a seriously compromised citizen. Since the appearance of the Command was recent, whether the disappearances were permanent was unclear; but most citizens assumed they were.

Cosmo had said, "No one knows why they don't just kidnap the citizens they want to question or kill or whatever they are doing to them. Why bother to compromise them?" He moodily ordered another bourbon. The urge to know what was going on was depressing and dangerous, but it could be profitable.

Brightening a little, Cosmo added, "I think I know a member of the Command. I was in a club the other night when a woman came in who instantly made everyone nervous.

"The club is on the side of the city where the rich people sometimes come to drink and party with the less fortunate. Also, some specialized services are available there, ones that are not available through sanctioned businesses. People with those tastes tend to be high strung and sensitive.

"I assumed it was a local digger that had everyone go silent. But the bartender, a guy I know from the army, said she wasn't a digger, that she had just appeared recently. The bartender was himself really nervous at the presence of this woman, who sat in the middle of the bar, perhaps by accident, but also perhaps so she could see the entire bar in the mirror.

She didn't hang her head over her drink, but looked around alertly. The bartender leaned over and whispered to me that he had heard she was a member of the Command."

Cosmo paused and Arlo sensed that the point of the story was coming.

"The thing is, I know her. At least I'm pretty sure she was a girl who lived in my old neighborhood. We went to school together for a few years; then she moved. The building she lived in was falling apart, and her parents must have found a better apartment. I always got along with her."

Successful diggers were very personable. It was part of their job description. Disarming might be the best word to describe the successful digger. A target knew what the digger was, but he or she was so disarming, so non-threatening, so downright friendly that the mark decided this nice person must be looking for someone else to turn in.

Arlo wanted more details about the potential Command member, but Cosmo was vague. Her name was, or had been when she was a young girl, Remy, but he could not remember her last name. He didn't know where she lived, but thought it remotely possible he could locate her parents.

And he could not remember the location of the club where he saw her.

"I might have been a little high," he conceded.

Arlo thought the Command might be the source of the rumor about Ana and Colt. And if this woman was in the Command, she might know what was going on.

What did Cosmo want in exchange for going to the trouble of tracking Remy, looking for her parents, being nice to them, checking out her neighborhood, possibly placing himself in harm's way? Arlo offered him a large bounty on a bad guy the authorities were looking for.

5

Remy Clon was surprised when Cosmo Naftali approached her in a club near her apartment. She recognized him instantly. He had always been handsome and she had had a little crush on him as a young girl. As she remembered, he was tremendously easy to talk with. Unfortunately she was a woman of secrets now.

"Remy," Cosmo had seated himself next to her on a bar stool, "How nice to see you. You are more beautiful than ever."

"I'm not beautiful, Cosmo. How nice to see you. I thought you were in the army." Remy felt flustered and unsure of herself. Would Irene be angry with her for talking with an old friend?

Cosmo thought she was looking quite prosperous; her hair, always her best feature, was cut short in a stylish way and her hands were well cared for. But she appeared haggard, with dark circles and a pinched look.

"Bring me up to date on what you've been doing since you moved out of the neighborhood. Did you go to university?" Cosmo watched her in the dark mirror behind the bar. Mirrors were banned under the N.D. The C.E. said they contributed to soul loss, and whatever that was, it was bad, but clubs and cafes generally ignored the ban. They argued that using dark mirrors both added to the atmosphere and lessened the opportunity for soul loss.

Remy fidgeted with the few things on the bar in front of her, including a comm jack she had apparently taken out of her ear and laid on the table.

"I was in the army. You remember, my father was in the army."

"I had forgotten," Cosmo said simply. "I remember being sad that you moved away. It seemed sudden."

Remy took a deep breath, rushing into speech. She had a babyish voice. "It was sudden. One day we were happy in our home, my mother and I. The next day we are rushing around packing a few things, my school things, a few of my bearsies."

Her eyes took on a haunted look, probably for the bearsies she had to leave behind. "We went to the desert. My father was the head of an army unit in the desert, and he wanted us with him. We had a new home. My Aunt Kathleen, my father's sister, came to live with us. When my mother died, she stayed and took care of me."

"I'm sorry to hear about your mother," Cosmo said.

"I didn't know my father thought she was having an affair. He brought her to the desert to get her away from the city and brought his sister to watch her while he was away on patrols. It was terrible for her. I was in school. I didn't know what was happening to her. I only found out afterward, after she killed herself."

"Oh, Remy, I'm so sorry." Cosmo was genuinely moved at the sadness of the story and the bereft tone in Remy's voice. He tried, unsuccessfully, to picture Remy's parents but no images came to mind. He had found her through his parents, who remembered only that the father had been in the army and away from home. In fact, Cosmo's father was not certain he had ever met him. Cosmo's parents knew Remy's Aunt Kathleen and, through her, located Remy's whereabouts in the city.

"She was never having an affair. No evidence was ever found. Aunt Kathleen never saw her do anything unfaithful. In fact, she was regretful about how she had treated my mother. Too late." She smiled sadly.

"I know I am bitter. My mother was so unhappy in the desert. Before, in the city, she had been so wonderful. We were good friends. We drew pictures together, and she told me stories of the animals in the olden days. Then in the desert, no one would talk to her even though her husband was the commander of the base. There were no jobs for her to get her out of the house, and my aunt was there all the time, watching her.

"I was in school. I didn't notice."

"You were a kid."

Cosmo was pleased with the direction the conversation was taking. Remy's mother's suicide was obviously something she thought about constantly and for which she was carrying guilt. In his experience, people laboring under such emotions were more vulnerable to subtle questioning, more open to blabbing.

"Your Aunt Kathleen turned out to be a good guy? She regretted being mean to your mother?"

"Yes. After Mama died, Aunt Kathleen got Mama's journals out of storage and went through them. She often said she was sorry she had waited, but she was only reading my mother's current journals when she was in the desert. From the old journals, it was clear my mother only loved my father and missed him when he was away."

"I'll bet your father was sad, too," Cosmo said, although he doubted it.

"No. He was very angry and said Aunt Kathleen was making excuses for her failure to find out who the man was and to keep my mother from killing herself."

"I'll bet he felt guilty and hid it with anger."

"Maybe," Remy said somberly, "but he sent us away to a little town on the coast and got another wife. I don't see him very much."

Cosmo ordered another round. It occurred to him that she must already be drunk to be saying these things.

"I've never seen the ocean." Cosmo said, sadly. "When I was in the army we were stationed in the mountains most of the time."

"I was stationed near the Conclave." She said it softly. "I did some intelligence work. Nothing important." By this, Cosmo inferred she had been a military concubine.

Remy was sitting near the end of the bar, and Cosmo had placed himself around the corner where he could watch her profile. Now he moved to the seat next to her, taking some nuts from the dish in front of her as a reason for the move.

The bartender, in conversation at the other end of the bar, ignored both of them. The club was nearly empty, the few customers either serious drinkers or engaged in intense conversations.

Remy nervously ran her hand through her beautiful hair, which smelled to Cosmo of a heavy flowery fragrance that reminded him of passion and damp sheets. He looked at her more carefully, searching for sensual signals, but he detected nothing. If necessary, he could use sex to obtain the information he wanted.

Remy fiddled with the clasp on her necklace, then rubbed the side of her finger over her thumb nail. Her eyes were shielded, far away.

Cosmo leaned in, almost whispering, willing his breath to brush her cheek. "You seem unhappy. Are things going badly for you since you left the service?" he murmured.

Such was his skill that she was not thrown out of her reverie by an intimate question from this person she had not seen in years, almost a stranger, coming into this club out of nowhere.

"Everything," she whispered back. "Everything is wrong. I'm in love, and love is wrong, isn't it? They say they love me, but they don't. If they did, they wouldn't treat me this way, make me do things."

Intriguing questions were surging through Cosmo's mind, but he dared not break the spell. Remy nervously drank from the nearly empty glass and bent a plastic stick back and forth, back and forth.

"Sometimes love is difficult," Cosmo prodded,

looking for the right tone.

"My love is not difficult. It is they who are difficult, they who say they want me, then push me away."

"Has it been a long time?" he asked.

"No, just since I came back to the city. I met Irene the first week I was here, at work. I was immediately attracted to her somehow. She was so helpful to me, new as I was. She immediately identified me as a Pagan, and that's forbidden. She said she was too." She suddenly stopped, stricken, and looked at Cosmo. "You won't say anything, will you? We could get in a lot of trouble."

"Never," Cosmo said. "What does it matter that you are Pagans?" His knowledge of Pagans was nonexistent at present, but he would tuck the information away for future research.

"Exactly. It is irrelevant to outsiders. To those of us inside, it is important. That's the way it is with all the religions. I know the C.E. are opposed, but really it is a personal decision."

"Many religious don't feel that way," he said.

"No. I know, I know." She sighed. "The pagan beliefs, they are simple, they require respect. But Irene does not respect me. I know it, but I can't help myself. And they make me do this work, this work I hate."

"Oh, what work is that?" Cosmo was holding his breath but his tone, he thought, was warm and trustworthy.

At that moment, the shift changed. The bartender stood up from the end of the bar and moved quickly to where they were seated, taking cash tokens. The flurry of activity awakened Remy, and she jumped off the stool.

Cosmo lost his cool for a moment, grabbed her arm. "What work is it?" What work are you talking about?"

She looked at his hand on her arm, frightened. "The Command," she said, "the Command," and fled.

6

Cosmo waited a minute, then slipped out of the club, catching sight of Remy as she hurried toward a nearby cluster of large apartment buildings lived in by well-off professionals and their families. The streets were moderately busy, so he had no trouble following her. She walked with her head down, oblivious to her surroundings. He watched her turn into the lobby of one of the multistory buildings, one thankfully without a doorman, and waited until he thought she had left the lobby. He strolled in casually and found the lobby was empty, the security device seemingly turned off. He scanned the listing of tenants—as with most of these buildings, it was half empty—and found nothing for Remy nor anyone named Irene, although there was a listing for an I. Thorne in the penthouse wing.

Stymied, he returned to the club. The bartender, now off duty, was having a drink alone at a table near the front of the almost empty club. Cosmo introduced himself and offered to buy him a drink. The bartender, a sad-faced person in his 50s, wrinkled, like a slightly deflated doll, pointed to a seat. "You don't have to buy. I get free drinks here." He waited for Cosmo to state his business. "Name's Huston." His name tag said Desi. Huston saw Cosmo looking at it. "Some things are need-to-know."

"Okay, Huston, what do you know about the girl I was drinking with earlier?"

"Not much. Her name is Remy. She comes in here pretty regular, sometimes with an older woman name of Irene. They seem to argue a lot, not be on the best terms. I think maybe an aunt or something." He winked and Cosmo didn't know if it was a tic or a message.

"Irene Thorne?" Cosmo asked.

The bartender looked interested, seemed to inflate a little. "If she's Irene Thorne, she's bad news. I never heard her last name in here. I took her for a lawyer or business type. A typical upper-class type."

"What's the deal with Irene Thorne? I just heard her name somewhere." Cosmo asked.

Huston leaned in. "I don't want to get into any trouble. I don't know you, you know, Cosmo." He put a little derision into the name, but Cosmo ignored it and pushed a cash token under the napkin next to Huston's drink.

Huston seemed satisfied. "I have a friend who works at one of the private clubs that caters to very highly placed political types, extremely rich people and connected. The club is very exclusive, and the customers really drink, falling-down drunk sometimes. My friend hears a lot of stories. Lately he's been hearing stories about some group called the

Command or something like that. The customers are very nervous about this group. My friend thinks they might be some kind of old-style gangsters, the kind we don't have any more."

Huston paused, took a drink, which gave Cosmo the opportunity to look around, see if anyone new had come in or if anyone was paying attention to their table.

"So far these bad guys, whether they are bad guys working for themselves or for the C.E., haven't shaken anyone down for money, at least as far as my friend has heard, but people whom they have shown an interest in seemed to disappear. Diggers don't bother the club's clientele—they are too protected. But this new group seems to find a way of getting at them because when the people disappear no one in authority seems to care. It will get around that they were engaged in serious unsanctioned behaviors. There are no investigations, no trials, public or otherwise, as far as anyone knows. People assume the whispers are true and people are nervous. Everyone engages in unsanctioned behaviors of some sort."

"Irene Thorne," Cosmo prodded.

Huston took another drink. "I'm getting to that. My friend says that the discussions have increased lately. More people are talking about the Command and recently they began mentioning that Irene Thorne may be connected with the group. She is a lawyer who worked mostly for the city and has a reputation for being tough and maybe even lethal. People who cross her go on permanent vacations."

"But what's her connection to the Command?"

"That's the question. My friend doesn't know, and he thinks his customers don't either. Somehow her name got connected with this group."

"That could be dangerous for her," Cosmo said.

"Maybe it's just a rumor or a coincidence. Maybe these people disappeared, and then someone mentioned the Command after the fact, like, as an excuse. Maybe someone heard a different someone at an adjacent table say Irene Thorne had great legs and confused the two conversations." Huston made a face that said, "You never know," stood up, stretched and picked up the cash token.

"Stop in again, Cosmo," he said.

Cosmo sat for a little while, thinking. It surprised him that Huston had heard of the Command and that he had been so extremely forthcoming. The cash token Cosmo had slipped under the napkin was not that big. Was he trying to find out whether Cosmo had heard of the Command or trying to get a line on who Cosmo was working for? Who was he working for? Cosmo was trying to figure *that* out himself. At the moment, it seemed he was working for Arlo, and dangerous work could be lucrative.

Teegan and Jordi worked at clubs on opposite corners of a central intersection in the entertainment district. Access points to the Subs were everywhere in this area so intrepid or foolish citizens could visit downside for a night's special entertainment. Most citizens stayed away from the Subs, but some were driven by necessity for goods and services only available downside, and in others, the desire for sensation eclipsed good sense. Working in close proximity to each other allowed Teegan and Jordi to meet at various times throughout the evening and to have dinner together some evenings at one or another of the cafes in the area. Teegan's club served food that was perfunctory at best, and Jordi's sold nothing but items designed to sponge up alcohol.

Both could have free meals at work, but The Rent Free, a quiet café with better than average food, was usually their choice. Tonight they were at a table in the back of the small dining room near the kitchen, where they could chat with the owner during lulls. On this particular evening, the evening after the digger was killed in the alley behind Sandy's, the café was unusually crowded.

Jordi had tried to talk about the incident several times, but Teegan refused to discuss it.

"I don't know why you keep talking about this. It had nothing to do with us. That we were in the alley just then was a coincidence. The kid was spying on someone else, smelled the smoke, and came back to see if he could pick up anything. After we went back inside, whoever he was looking to sell to the authorities found him and killed him. End of story." She held up a menu. "Come on. Let's order. I'm starved." She studied the menu.

"It just bothers me," Jordi's voice held a whining tone.

"What bothers you?"

"That chopstick. Why stab someone with a chopstick. It seems so brutal." And, Jordi thought, it was a chopstick like the one you were using not two hours before, a chopstick, moreover, that disappeared from the garbage.

"It seems obvious to me that the killer either did not have another weapon or was smart enough to realize that a thin plastic chopstick is just as good as a stiletto any day. Maybe the killer had military training or was from the Subs. All kinds of people live in the Subs. I don't know, and I don't care. Anything can happen to diggers. It's a dangerous occupation."

They both ordered stuffed portabellas from the owner's granddaughter although they knew she might bring them anything. She was new at waiting and didn't know the menu.

"Do you think he was following Pel?" Jordi could not leave it alone.

"Probably. Pel seemed like he had a lot of things happening in his life. You know getting caught smoking will result in major time in a re-education camp. Personally, I hope never to see him again."

"At least he told us about Ana and Colt being sought by someone in the Subs."

"For what good it did us. We know Arlo is back from wherever he went when he got in trouble, and we know that Arlo has both friends and enemies in the city and probably elsewhere. So are Ana and Colt being sought by Arlo or by friends of Arlo or enemies of Arlo or by someone entirely different? And if so, who? The whole mess gives me a headache. We don't know any more than we did." Teegan forked moodily at her portabellas and rice.

"I just wish Arlo had stayed away. I love the guy but. . ." Teegan left the comment hanging as the waiter brought the bitter green salad she had forgotten previously.

"Oh, are you talking about Arlo Gauss?" the girl said brightly—and loudly.

Teegan and Jordi were shocked. She banged the salads into small open spaces on the table and topped off their wine glasses, chattering happily.

"Oh, he is such a hero. It's a shame he had to

leave the city and could not stay and take credit for his work."

"I thought he was in trouble with the C.E.," Teegan said doubtfully while looking at Jordi to shut the girl up.

"Oh, yes. But that was a misunderstanding. It would have been cleared up."

Jordi started to stand up, to put his hand over the girl's mouth, if necessary, but her grandfather rushed over, urging her to take care of her other customers who were demanding service.

"I am so sorry," he apologized to Teegan and Jordi. "She is new in town and doesn't understand our ways." He rushed off.

Teegan and Jordi finished their meal in silence. The girl should be sent back to the country before she fell prey to a digger or worse.

7

Linnet overturned a box and sat down behind a dumpster to think about the next steps her life should take. She ate a protein bar she had bought in the Subs. They were strange people but mostly nice to her. Colt and other people didn't know she had friends there, friends she had met after he had helped her. Linnet didn't know what to do about Colt, how she felt about him. Her experience with males was so limited; at home, she only interacted with her father and, when she came of age, with Oren. Colt was nice looking, although that wasn't supposed to be important, blond with grey eyes, maybe a little narrow, the eyes. And he was strong. He had told her he did a martial art. She didn't know what that was and could not remember the name. Obviously it left him tight and muscular. Handsome, she admitted, he was handsome. Could she trust him? She had no criteria for judging.

She sighed inwardly. The men at Heartsease were

not handsome. Being farmers, they were rather fat and only their faces were tanned. The rest of their bodies were pasty and unpleasant. Her mother and the older women were always talking about how appearance, concern for appearance, was frivolous and demeaning. But the girls all talked about the few men they saw at the weekly assemblies in terms of their looks. Only the chief elder's son was really handsome, and he was beyond the aspirations of any of the farm girls. The older women said he would probably go away to university—as a child she'd had not idea what that meant—then come back and pick the prettiest girl for a wife. He might even bring a girl from the chaotic outside world, give her shelter in Heartsease.

Linnet mentally kicked herself for dwelling on the past. Now that she had left the community she could not go back. Once you left, you were dead to them. Most folks assumed you were just dead, period.

Now she knew that the world outside the community was nothing like the one preached by the patriarchs and elders.

She had reached the city pretty much as Oren had unwittingly suggested, hiding in a truck filled with vegetables. Once the truck stopped and the driver left, she was able to creep out of what appeared to be a warehouse and into the streets of the city. Here she had been stymied. The buildings and vehicles were unlike anything she had imagined. The people were all kinds and colors, all dressed in the drab pants and tops that passed as the city uniform. Even the women wore pants, something strictly forbidden in the community. Her first task was to outfit herself in the uniform; for that, she had stolen a few cash tokens from the truck where the driver had conveniently left them. They didn't last long though, and she had been down to a very few, after becoming outfitted to blend in with the rest of the citizens in grey pants and shirt.

She had not been able to cut her hair. She could not find it within herself to commit such a major sin, but she saw very few women with long hair. And, at the secondhand clothing store, she had noticed the counterman had eyed it covetously. She could, he said, get good money for it. He offered to be her agent, but she declined. He had said, "I guess you're heading for the Subs. Take a tip from me and hide your hair. Someone will take it from you." He tossed a dirty knit cap in her direction and she backed out, terrified. That had been the first time she had heard of the Subs.

As she wandered through the city, entranced by its magnitude and diversity, she had gravitated to the sections with smaller buildings and lots of busy little shops and clubs. She had had a supply of protein bars hidden under her new secondhand shirt, but became low on cash tokens. The older sections of the city had lots of alleys and places to hide through the nights.

Day and night in the city was different from day and night in the country. The sky was darker overall so that full daylight occurred for only a few hours. Clouds obscured the stars so that the night sky was a featureless void. Even the myriad satellites were invisible to her. It left a strange sensation, as though she had fallen into a deep hole.

Her supply of protein bars had slowly vanished as had her cash coins. Linnet had begun to feel desperate, her gift for effacing herself in the city proving mixed; she felt safer, but she made no friends. She doubted her ability to judge whether people were friendly. The people she met had edges to them that Heartsease people lacked. At least there, as long as you did not run afoul of the leadership, you were safe. Here she felt in danger every moment.

In desperation she had searched for the secondhand clothing store where the counterman had offered to broker the sale of her hair, but she could not find it again.

She had tried to think of ways to make friends, get work, but she was so depleted physically and emotionally that all she could do was cry. When she had been at the end—the money gone, the food gone, hungry and alone—she thought about ways to end her life. Her horror at the enormity of the transgression against the C.E. dwindled. Suicide, citizens whispered the word, was a sin of sins. Maybe words didn't matter. She was starving to death.

That had been her condition when Colt had found her one night, coming back from gaming. She was sitting on a garbage can, crying, her long hair, now filthy, hanging from under her cap.

He had approached her warily, knowing she might be a gang decoy, but her tears fell so feebly, she was so bereft, so lost, that he had approached her.

To Linnet, in his blond handsomeness, he had seemed an hallucination. She thought, *I am finally going to die; this is the angel of death.* Yet he spoke to her in a normal voice, asked her name, said he was called Colt. He seemed solid, vital.

He asked her gently if she was hungry, and she had nodded, hopelessly. Could she walk? Well, yes but not very well. So he helped her into a small diner and brought her a cup of miso soup, her first, then some soft noodles and tea.

He didn't ask her questions, rather watched her closely, relaxed and intent, through narrow grey eyes. He was wearing what she recognized as a form of the city uniform, ill-fitting pants and a baggy shirt, disguising his tight muscular form. As her blood sugar came up, she noticed, with chagrin, how dirty her hands were.

Slowly she told him about herself, about the community, about Heartsease. He asked her few questions and was especially concerned that she did not have a city permit and ID disc. Without those she was liable to be picked up and dumped in the countryside.

"We need to find you a place to stay," he said, "and a city permit."

Before anything else, he took her to a bathhouse, gave the attendant a cash token. The attendant helped her figure out how to clean herself and her hair, how to put her clothes in a sanitizer. After that, Linnet felt almost reborn, with some food and clean clothes. She began to be suspicious of Colt, the stranger who picked her up.

The bath attendant was motherly, helping her get dressed, patting her on the shoulder, braiding her hair and tucking it under the now clean cap.

"You must have gotten yourself in a mess," she remarked. "You can't keep living on the streets. You'll get picked up by the authorities or turned in by a digger. Your boyfriend needs to go to the Subs and buy you a city permit, too."

She handed Linnet a cord necklace, instructed her to wear it around her neck, and tucked into her shirt. "It looks like you've got an identity disc."

When she emerged from the bathhouse, Colt was waiting for her. "I have a place you can stay for a few days while we figure out what to do with you."

She had thought about protesting but, having no recourse, followed meekly as Colt led her to a club where he spoke briefly to the bartender, then led her to the back and up a flight of stairs, card-keying a door to reveal a small bedroom with an attached bath.

"The bartender's name is Mauritz. He keeps this place for himself when he's too tired to go home," Colt said. "You can use it for a few days. I've fixed it up with him to give you meals downstairs. Don't stay down there too long, and don't go outside until I get you a city permit and ID disc."

She had been spiraling down into exhaustion and at that moment could only say thank you again and again while falling asleep on the first soft bed in a long time.

The next morning, she had gone downstairs and introduced herself to Mauritz, the owner, manager, and bartender, a big graceful man with a way of talking like everything he said was a secret. The club was not busy just then, and he went into the kitchen, returning with a pot of tea, two cups, and pastries, which he placed before her with a pat on her shoulder.

He had sat down opposite her and helped himself to a cup of tea. Linnet expected he would pester her with questions, but instead he began telling her about Colt, whom he had known for several years. He and Colt practiced in the same dojo. He told her about Colt's wife, Ana, a professor at the university, and stressed, Linnet thought quite kindly, that Colt was a very good person and devoted to Ana.

Eventually she and Mauritz became friends and she confided her story of the escape from the community, stressing that she would not be able to return. She told him about her marriage to Oren and how he had inadvertently helped her escape. Mauritz was concerned that Oren might follow her, something Linnet had never considered.

The hours when Linnet had to keep out of sight in Mauritz's little room upstairs were long, boring ones which she spent watching videos and sleeping. Occasionally she would help Mauritz's wife, Janine, with the cooking. But the kitchen was tiny, and Janine, a petite woman much younger than her husband, was not happy to have her help.

The question exercising Colt and Linnet and Mauritz was discussed at length—what would Linnet do now that she was in the city. She would need to work, difficult without training or references. Janine said she could not cook and she lacked the city-bred alertness to be a waiter.

Ultimately the decision was made to approach a distant cousin of Mauritz who could employ her as a sex worker. The cousin operated a sanctioned sex shop called The House of Blue Leaves that catered mostly to older professionals. Mauritz assured Linnet that the work was easy, and the proprietor was a fair and honest person. Linnet would be trained first in the four basic sanctioned modes of sex work and, if she enjoyed the work, be trained in the other, more esoteric, more profitable, modes. Even the four basic modes of sex work paid well and she could live in a residential hotel that catered to the other sex workers.

The idea repulsed her; she had hated providing sex for Oren, and now she was forced to perform abhorrent acts with strangers. She tried to talk to Janine about her concerns, but Janine was dismissive. "It's easy work; one, two customers a night, and the pay is good. Customers of The House of Blue Leaves are older and more cultivated than houses catering to younger, more vigorous people. Be grateful you will not be providing services for the port workers."

So Linnet had become a sex worker at The House of Blue Leaves, and, as Janine had foretold, the work was easy. She was introduced to the four basic modes of sex work by the proprietor Sparrow, who projected a warm, grandmotherly appearance but, as Linnet found, was a functioning male. Sparrow was unhappy with Linnet's performance, which he described as perfunctory, but he felt sorry for her and he was especially pleased with her long hair for which an extra fee could be charged.

His attitude had changed one day when she sought him out in the café. On most days the café doubled as his office where he could keep an eye on the business, drink endless cups of tea, and chat with the boys and girls. Sparrow took a personal interest in the kids who worked for him as sex workers and for his other staff. He was naturally kind and hated to be harsh, even as it was sometime necessary. With Linnet he always felt slightly off base. Her excessive defensiveness, coupled with her apparent fear of him, left him uncomfortable.

When he saw her approach, he felt a flutter of concern. She never approached him if she could help it.

She was wearing the house uniform, a kind of white toga with strategic slits, but despite the warmth, she looked cold and physically out of sorts. She perched on the seat next to him.

"Linnet, darling, you look tired. Let me get you some tea." He ignored her head shake and waved for the waiter.

For her part, Linnet hated approaching him, because, although he was unfailingly kind, she knew she was inadequate at her work because she hated it.

"I, I need to talk to you." She had tried to get Virginia, who was a kind of house mother to the girls, to speak for her but Virginia, who loved Sparrow, said airily, "Just talk to him, sweetie. He'll understand. He won't hurt you."

She had sat carefully, pulling her toga around her body. Sparrow felt mildly exasperated at her timidity. On the other hand, maybe he could make something of it. Some people, especially their elderly clientele, might be attracted by this girlish reticence. He envisioned putting her in a more traditional outfit. Something referencing the peasantry. The C.E. had made much of the innocence of the peasantry. He could pipe in some flutes and bells. While he mulled over opportunities to take advantage of her shyness, Linnet suffered in silence, trying to think of the appropriate words to explain her problem. His uncharacteristic delay in speaking left her more nervous.

"I, I can't work today. I'm sick," she finally said.

Sparrow leaned forward, suddenly concerned, taking her hand. "You should have told Virginia. She's in charge of the assignments today. She could have called a healer."

"Oh, I don't need a healer." Linnet was suddenly confident. "I just need a day or two without. . .you know. . .working. Then I'll be fine. I did tell Virginia, but she said I should tell you."

This interested Sparrow. Virginia was reliable. She would not waste his time with a minor malady without reason.

"What is your problem, darling?" His tone was a shade peremptory.

Linnet blushed and fiddled with her toga. "I'm having my monthly. . ." she paused again, unsure of the proper terminology with a man, even one who looked like a woman.

"You have monthly bleeding?" he said, enlightened.

She nodded, looking at her lap.

"Every month?"

"Oh, no. Not every month." She didn't want him to think she would be unable to work every month. She had to be honest, though. "Most months."

"But you are not worried about getting pregnant."

"I have an implant. They gave it to me when I started. . .you know. . .and would have removed it when it was time."

"Time for you to become a surrogate."

"We don't have surrogates; they're immoral." Linnet clarified with the hint of smugness she used when talking about her former community. "At least not when we are first in a sanctioned relationship. Sometimes I guess after that, if the C.E. think it is necessary, sometimes." Sparrow detected a hint of reticence in Linnet. As if she realized she was saying too much.

"Are there many fertile women in your community?"

"Quite a few. Most of us were from the North." For some reason the effects of the plague had been less pronounced in the northern countries.

"So there must be lots of children. So different from the cities." He tried to look sad.

Linnet did look sad. "Well, no, you get to keep the first one, of course. But the others are put in the crèches outside the community. The C.E. say we cannot support that many children. A lot of the mothers are unhappy, but it's better for the children, I guess." She didn't look convinced.

"And what is your reward for having these children?"

Linnet looked blank. "Reward?"

Sparrow changed the subject.

"You need a cup of tea." He spoke to the waiter who had been patiently waiting for their order. "Bring Linnet a cup of my special slipleaf tea. It will ease her pain."

And open her mouth, the waiter thought silently; slipleaf tea was a strong natural painkiller with the side effect of releasing inhibitions. Whatever Sparrow wanted to know, she would tell him.

Linnet had settled into her new life in the city. Sparrow was working to get her a legitimate city permit and ID disc, and Linnet was saving money. Her performance improved somewhat, and she had became popular with elderly patrons who enjoyed a less active style. She offered both Colt and Mauritz money in repayment for their hospitality, but they both declined. With Sparrow's approval, she shyly offered both of them free services, but these they also declined, to her relief. Colt did not patronize the sex shop, but often came to check on her at the club that was part of the House's business. He had even visited her in her room at the residential hotel that catered to the House staff, but he showed no signs of personal interest in her.

Now she had made friends in the city and had lucrative work. She often saw Mauritz and even Janine, who had become more friendly now that Linnet was living elsewhere. The other sex workers were also friendly. Sparrow tried to create a family atmosphere for his young staff and, aside from the natural arrogance of the upper level workers, whose specialized services were more expensive and flamboyant, largely succeeded.

She became especially close to a boy named Roman who helped her begin training in some second-level modes, but she was still lonely. Roman was married to a sex worker in another house, and they intended one day to open an affiliate house in another part of the city. Most of the kids had connections in the Subs, and she had become friendly with some of the inhabitants downside.

Then, one evening, sitting at the house bar, trying to learn the contents of various aphrodisiac cocktails from Dodie, the bartender, Irene Thorne came into the House of Blue Leaves, and for Linnet, it had been the beginning of a nightmare.

Now she was embroiled in a life she could never have imagined and did not know where to turn, who she could trust. She could not confide in her friends in the Subs, and she was unsure about Colt and Ana. As she sat behind the dumpster, she was almost nostalgic for her life in Heartsease.

8

Ana was dressed more carefully than usual and trying not to fidget in her seat at a conference concerning *Materialist Education for Non-Academic Citizens.* The university had mounted the conference to discuss responses to the increasing number of citizens and intellectuals who were concerned about the fragility of the physical universe. In Ana's view, most citizens were ignorant and badly educated; that through the silly alarmist propaganda of the protesters, they were being infected with a particularly virulent idea. Unfortunately, that idea, if pursued to its ultimate extreme, was eradication of all non-materialist research and speculation and would significantly affect the work she and the professor were doing at the institute and, more frightening to consider, could put them in personal danger. The protesters' threats against Dr. Elvistine were being captioned by the city Authorities as baseless posturing. Ana was not convinced.

She and Elvistine had been forced to attend this conference by the university president. Elvistine and the Institute of Temporal Epistemology, more usually just called ITE, were high profile and the president wanted Elvistine on public view as a representative of the university.

Although part of the school, accessible for classes and symposia by students and faculty, and drawing talented mathematicians and theoretical physicists from the student population, ITE was independently funded with support flowing from the Conclave of Elders and from numerous business and industrial interests. The identities of the latter were known only to the professor. As a result, no one could influence Dr. Elvistine in hiring, teaching, or choice of projects. A constant source of conflict with the trustees of the university was his disinclination to publicly disseminate progress reports and findings.

Ana had been trying to convince the professor to separate ITE from the university completely. She thought if they could pursue their studies in anonymity, delivering results directly to the sponsors and not be forced to publicize their findings, which were misunderstood by nearly everyone, they would be safe.

Dr. Elvistine did not want to separate from the university which provided free support and services plus access to talented technicians. He was convinced that the support of the Conclave meant they were untouchable. Ana doubted the C.E. could act fast enough if the protesters turned into a mob and started attacking the buildings of the institute. Ever larger groups of protesters were gathering periodically to trumpet their fear of untethered thought, whatever that was. The valence of new ideas terrified them, especially ideas that involved the foundations of the universe. The discovery and apparent reality of a parallel universe had spooked citizens, many of whom were still secretly religious. Rather than embracing the discovery, so at odds with their various religious cosmologies, they blamed the university for the existence of the alternate universe, as though the effort to make contact itself caused its existence.

Many thinkers at the highest levels of the Conclave of Elders had denounced the irrationality of the idea, pointing to the solid reality of the universe. They would say things like, "You use a hammer to break a rock, not a picture of a hammer," but a large portion of the populace was not convinced.

Citizens had experienced the emergence of the New Dispensation almost magically flowing from the idea of one ruler of the planet to its actuality in a matter of a decade. Parents and grandparents remembered how the idea had seemed fantastical, "Utopian" was a word often used in those days, and then before their eyes, it had come to pass. Their belief in the solidity and predictability of the material world had been shattered.

At the moment, Ana was struck by the solidity of the president of the university, a square man in a flowing black gown. Elvistine, sitting next to her, was fiddling with his cuticles and making notes on a piece of plastic with an old fashioned ballpoint pen. Elvistine was a small, pudgy man, wearing a dusty black suit of some sort of stretchy material and sporting a white scarf. The scarf was an affectation that verged on illegal frivolity.

On the podium, the president was concluding his

inconclusive remarks, and the audience applauded politely. Elvistine stuck his notes in his backpack and rose, waiting impatiently for the row to empty. The attendees stood around in little groups, and no one spoke to Elvistine and Ana as they exited. Their status was anomalous among the faculty. Elvistine was famous for his discoveries in quantum physics even before his revelation of the portal between the universes. A certain amount of envy was tempered with self- preservation. Under the N.D., fame was an uncertain commodity. While providing access to money and patronage for projects and a modicum of protection from the authorities, famous citizens who uttered a hint of criticism would often suffer public revelations of social crimes followed by trips to long-term re-education facilities. Furthering a career involved walking a fine line.

Besides being an object of envy, the institute was mysterious. The ample funding for equipment and space, the munificent stipends for the brightest students, generated dangerous gossip. The institute was located inside a high fence at the edge of the campus, accessible only with a special pass. At the moment, Ana and Elvistine were approaching the gate in a fast little air sled coveted by those trudging on foot or by bicycle across the vast campus.

The facility was a classic white cube with a dome, also white; the few windows covered with a coating that rendered them almost invisible. A high, featureless wall enclosed the building. As they approached the gate, it opened automatically, and they wafted through. Elvistine jumped out of the air sled and charged into the foyer, followed by Ana.

The structure was hollow with rows of cubicles

lining three sides. Silvery light filtered through the dome, interrupted by almost invisible girders to form a pattern like a lotus on the floor.

Colt was standing in the middle of the room, his backpack slung over his shoulder, directly under the apogee of the dome, talking with one of the institute staff.

Dr. Elvistine greeted him warmly, shaking hands and commenting on the weather, making small talk. Ana approached her husband less enthusiastically, giving him a perfunctory peck on the cheek.

"What are you doing here?" she asked.

"We can't talk here. Let's go to your office."

Elvistine started to walk away, and Colt said, "No, Professor, you come too. I want to take Ana away for a while, and we need your help."

The professor looked surprised, but nodded and preceded them into his office and work room, gesturing toward a little sitting area in the corner. They clustered around the low table while Elvistine picked up the intercom and asked for tea.

"What's this all about, Colt? Is it about Arlo?" Ana sounded irritated.

Colt turned to the professor. "You know that Ana and I were very close to Arlo Gauss at one time, before he got in trouble with the authorities and vanished."

The professor nodded, suddenly looking alert, even wary, Colt thought. Elvistine stopped looking directly at Colt and gazed into the distance, as if he thought Colt could read his mind through his eyes.

"Now Arlo has reappeared, at least reappeared in the Subs. We haven't seen him, but we have received word from various people that he wants to see Ana.

He was in love with Ana at one time and probably still is." Colt looked at her. "I can understand that."

Ana ignored him and stared at her hands, nested in her lap.

All three looked at the door as a student knocked briefly and entered with a tray holding a tea carafe, cups, and a little dish with the professor's favorite nuts. The student put the tray on a low table and, glancing questioningly at Colt, hurried out, closing the door quietly.

"Will he listen?" Colt asked the professor.

"Probably, but he's reliable," Elvistine said, helping himself to tea and nuts.

Colt poured out a cup for Ana and one for himself. "The point is, Arlo wants to see Ana, and I don't want her near him. Once he emerges from the Subs—and he will sooner or later, because Ana will not go there to see him—he'll seek her out." He glanced over at his wife to see if she agreed with him.

"Nothing and no one could get me into the Subs," she said.

"You see." Colt said to Elvistine. "So I want to take Ana somewhere safe until Arlo gets caught or returns to wherever he came from."

"How will you know when he leaves? He could hang out in the Subs for years."

"I'll know," Colt said. "I have my own contacts downside."

"Do you think the only reason he returned to the city was to see Ana?" The professor spoke, Colt thought, with a bit more emphasis than the question deserved.

"We have no way of knowing why he returned. He has interests in the Subs; business interests, I believe.

Also, he is a religionist; he has fellow religionists there."

"You don't know that for sure," Ana looked up suddenly, glancing meaningfully toward the door.

"I do know it for sure. And if Arlo were sent to a re-education facility for being religious, it would solve our problems."

Ana shuddered. "Those places are terrible."

"So you have some feelings for Arlo?" the professor said to Ana.

Ana shook her head, both irritated and defensive.

"Of course, I do. He is one of my oldest friends and a brilliant thinker."

"You don't think he's here because of our current project?" Elvistine asked. He started to say more, then suddenly seemed to remember the presence of Colt and stopped.

"Don't censor yourself on my account, Professor," Colt said. "I know about the time project."

Elvistine looked at Ana, accusingly, and started to remonstrate.

She raised a hand. "Don't say it, Desmond." Using his first name was a cautionary signal. "I was going to tell you when I got a chance. Colt heard about the time project from Chandler Besdine."

Elvistine was clearly disturbed. "Who?"

"I had forgotten him also, but I talked to the department secretary. She remembers everything. He worked with us on the astrology project, then became Tillman's protégé."

"The guy with the ball?" Elvistine made a gesture toward the back of his head and Colt nodded. "Oh, no." Elvistine jumped up and began pacing. "This is terrible. He was much more than Tillman's protégé, he was a believer in Tillman's theories. They were very close." Elvistine cross-examined Colt about where he had seen Chandler, how long previously. Had Chandler been around lately, or had he just appeared? As Colt talked, Elvistine became more agitated.

"I need to talk to Ara ben Semion, my contact in the Conclave, immediately. He'll need to know that Tillman is active once more, spying on me and our work at the institute. That is the only explanation for Chandler's comment to Colt. Tillman is sending a threat to me through Colt. Tillman was supposed to be silenced. Someone will have to go to ben Semion at once." He stopped pacing, unwrapped his white scarf and held the two ends wrapped around his hands like he was going to garrote someone, presumably Tillman.

Behind his back, Colt was sending Ana interrogative glances, but she shrugged, *I don't know.*

"That's it," Elvistine said decisively. "I must go to conclave headquarters at once and alert them that Tillman is still actively trying to sabotage our work. Ana you must come with me."

Ana opened her mouth, astounded, and Colt stood up and put his hand on her shoulder, "No, absolutely not. Ana is not going anywhere near the Conclave."

9

What is the strangest thing about love, the intensity of love, the objects of love, the fact that love is so often unpredictable, falling out of love and its consequent anguish? The C.E. had not addressed love in the New Dispensation, but they had tried to defuse the contretemps of sexual desire by making sex a commodity. Anyone could get any kind of sex they wanted for a price and the prices were, by and large, kept low. Only for the more esoteric and dangerous modes were the prices stratospheric, and they were accessible from real, not virtual, objects of desire.

However, these services did not satisfy everyone. For one thing, the participants were willing. For some citizens, the activity was less interesting if the other party or parties were willing. For those citizens with specialized tastes, brokers had emerged who could provide the required services, usually by luring and drugging homeless kids, who were plentiful in the Subs, into involuntary cooperation.

Piet Lem, the chieftain of Grupo Uno, hated these brokers. He took a personal interest in the kids who found themselves in the Subs. They were often citizens with gumption that he could use in his enterprises. They had taken a chance coming to the Subs, and Piet wanted to give them a chance to help themselves.

Piet was not a sadist. Such brokers who came to his attention, and were within his sphere of influence downside, would find themselves cut off from their protection, deprived of their weapons, and executed. Simple, neat, and efficient.

Piet's religion taught that they might or might not enjoy an afterlife in which to atone and join in the proper human activity of calling out and searching for Fong, the supreme God. Piet Lem himself meditated every day before the image of Isis/Osiris in their joint aspect, asking for guidance in the ongoing search for Fong, who was lost to himself, or at least to the people of this sphere.

Piet had very little idea of the physical structure of the world and the skies. In the old days, he knew there were savants who understood such things and even today in the universities there were such scholars. Among citizens, especially the unsanctioned of the Subs, the physical universe was a vague concept. All he knew was that the one supreme god they called Fong was lost to them, and possibly to himself, and their task was to awaken Fong to their plight as humans and possibly to its own existence as the prime deity.

So while Piet Lem did not enjoy killing citizens, if necessary, he would do it and not feel too bad in the bargain. Sending people to the re-education facilities, as the diggers did, was bad enough, but Piet usually left them alone to make a living. Forcing kids into degrading, harmful, and potentially lethal sex acts was unforgivable.

On this particular day, he was chatting with one such broker named Jonson who moved freely between the upside and downside. He had developed a considerable following downside because of his many illegal businesses, and Piet honored him for that and planned to allow Jonson's chief associate to continue those businesses as long as the associate understood that the brokering of kids to perverts was not an option.

Piet had run into a problem because Jonson was telling him about his family, a young wife and daughter. Jonson clearly and unambiguously loved his wife and child. He told Piet Lem far too many stories about cute things his daughter said and the wonderful activities he participated in with his wife and child. Piet was thinking to himself that he would have to ensure that Jonson's family was cared for even as he was unwillingly remembering the loss of his own father at a young age.

Piet's father had died protecting his books from the Conclave. His father had not believed that the paper sheltered a deadly virus that would kill them all if the books were not destroyed. He had not believed the stories told by the C.E. and thought this was their way of getting rid of the books, a prelude to mind control. Piet Lem's mother often explained that many people had shared his father's opinions but, like his father, that they had been wrong, because since the destruction of the books, no one had contracted the virus.

Piet Lem had followed Jonson to one of the upside clubs he favored and introduced himself as a friend of a friend. Jonson had bought a bottle of scotch and they had been working on it since. He talked and talked, but Piet Lem found himself liking him. How he could bring himself to do the things he did puzzled Piet, who thought himself a good judge of people.

As the evening progressed, Piet Lem alluded to Jonson's business within the sex trade. He allowed as how he was interested in getting involved himself because the business was so lucrative. Jonson was amused. "If you're interested in getting into the sex trade, you're better off going legit. Working the dark side is difficult. I learned it from my dad, who perfected some of the techniques. He gave me his list of customers when he retired."

Piet Lem wanted to know how his dad built up the list of customers. "I don't know," Jonson laughed. "It was before the N.D. The extreme services are a small part of my business. I can see that you are interested in the kinky stuff, and I hate to disappoint you, but I can't tell you how to do it. I do it my way which is complete theatre." He shook his head at Piet Lem's startled expression.

"I'm the most successful of the entrepreneurs downside because I don't just go out and kidnap some kid and expect them to perform. Most of the pervos have some fantasy they want to fulfill. They want to think they are bringing their partners to ecstasy against their will. They want to inflict pain because that heightens the experience for them. They don't stop to think that it doesn't work for the normal person. So we provide the experience. The customer doesn't know it is theatre. We don't let anyone get really hurt. Our kids are willing to put up with a certain amount of pain for the cash tokens. We can even simulate a snuff experience if the money is good."

He laughed. "I had one kid who could look terrified and yet vaguely hot at the same time. She was just excellent. Unfortunately, I married her, and I've never found a replacement." Piet Lem laughed with him.

"I won't help you if you are going to try the usual method, using drugs to force kids into the business. I don't know how to do it myself, and I would not consider it." Jonson took a reflective drink of scotch and shuddered. "If you want to adopt my methods," he continued, "you'll find your biggest challenge is getting a supply of young kids to train to do the work. Almost all the pervos want to work out on youngsters, so you need teens. And when they get too adept, the pervos sense it and it detracts from the experience. If they are really good, you have trouble reusing them. The pervos all want it to be the first time."

Piet Lem was bemused by Jonson's account. It made sense to him in a way because he had not encountered this aspect of Jonson's business until recently. Usually someone complained to him about a broker forcing kids to do real sex acts of the kind Jonson was faking. He had assumed Jonson was new on the scene, but his description of his dad rang some distant bells.

Jonson's other businesses were in a remote part of the Subs where they did not affect Piet's businesses.

Even as Piet Lem was trying to figure out what to

do with Jonson, he was pretty sure he was not going to execute him as planned. He sensed that something was weighing on Jonson's mind. His description of his family, for example, was tinged with a kind of desperation that puzzled Piet Lem. Finally, Jonson said sadly, "Everything was going well and now everything is just thoroughly cocked. I'm cocked, you're cocked, my family is cocked. And when I or die or disappear, which are the same thing, my wife will have to live with her mother, and her mother's an unsanctioned bitch."

"What do you mean? It sounds like you've got things under control." Piet Lem poured out a couple more drinks. Fortunately, he had taken anti-inebriation capsules. Jonson looked around, more obviously than if he had been sober, and lowered his voice. "It's these damned commandists, or whatever they are called. They have been destroying my little sideline business. My customers are disappearing, and no one is looking for them. They are all rich and protected, and yet they disappear and the authorities don't do anything. Also, some of the brokers that make most of their money from illegal sex have died."

"What are these? What did you call them. . . ?"

"I've heard them called commandists, commandos, all kinds of things. I don't know what they call themselves. I've never met one, seen one. All I've heard are rumors that go nowhere. The reality is, people on the upside are disappearing and people on the downside are dying."

"You think they are after you?" Piet Lem asked.

"That's what I heard." Jonson said. "I tried to track the rumor, but I got nothing. I'm a dead man," he said. "Let's have another drink."

"You think they are pursuing you because of your sideline?

"How do I know? The people I know who are disappearing are my customers, my pervos. I have to believe it has something to do with that. If you are interested, I can put you in touch with some of the kids who work for me. Maybe you can make some money before the whole business folds."

Piet Lem really liked Jonson, but he thought it prudent to distance himself. He pretended to be aware of the time and left Jonson to finish the scotch.

Piet Lem was more than usually alert to his surroundings when he left the club after his meeting with Jonson. He felt exposed, in danger, from this shadow group, these commandos. No one he knew had the kind of experiences Jonson described happening to his customers, but Arlo had brought the idea to him, that there was a group operating in the Subs that he was not aware of. And having spent practically his entire life downside, Piet Lem was worried.

If true, the theatre Jonson had described appealed to him. He liked the idea. You were providing an experience. True, the customer thought it was the real thing, but there was a lot of delusion in the N.D. Maybe the N.D. was itself a delusion; a culture of citizens trying to reify a fantasy, willfully pretending not to see.

10

Arlo met Cosmo at a bathhouse where they could get lost in the crowds of naked people, nothing being harder to identify than a citizen without clothes. They perched on the top shelf of a steam room where they could see the other customers. No one looked interested or interesting. One couple was obviously in love, and Arlo and Cosmo both wondered with amused detachment whether they would have sex right there. The guy was clearly ready.

Cosmo recounted his encounter with Remy and her semi-confession of working for a group she had identified as the Command. They both agreed that Irene Thorne needed to be investigated and kicked around different ideas. They still had no conception of the goal of the group, if it was a formal group, or if it was just a small band of disgruntled citizens who had found a way to deliver some personal justice.

"I have to think the group is connected with the authorities. Otherwise why would they want information on Ana and Colt to legitimate their disappearances. Why not just disappear them?" Arlo wondered.

"The bartender said people are disappearing, especially people who are in conflict with this Irene Thorne, but he didn't know whether there was a theme to the disappearances. You ever heard of Irene Thorne?" Cosmo asked.

"Never, but I plan to find out what I can. I need to get a look at her. Maybe I know her under another name."

"Remy lives with her, so that should provide an opportunity to see her. The neighborhood where they live is too open to surveil," Cosmo said. "I'll stop by the club and ask the bartender to get in touch with me when Irene Thorne arrives. He said she and Remy came in often."

The aroused man and his girlfriend had not made any progress toward a solution to his problem, so Arlo and Cosmo stepped around them and went through to the cold room. Refreshed, they went their separate ways, Cosmo to talk to the bartender and Arlo to talk with Piet Lem.

Exiting the bathhouse, Arlo immediately ducked into a subway station, one with a working train, and purchased a token from one of the kids hanging out. The barriers were long since non-functional so the kids were a kind of fail safe for the authorities that kept citizens from riding the subways for free. Unless you bought a token from them, you were apt to find yourself over the edge of the platform with a rat's eye view of the filth on the floor of the tunnels.

Arlo had no problems, however. He knew most of

the kids in this subway stop and went to stand in the shadows waiting for the train. Once on the train, he waited until he saw the green light of a maintenance niche, pulled a lever that slowed the train and opened the doors, and jumped into the niche. Although it appeared to be a solid wall, the niche opened into a corridor that accessed the Subs, and once there, Arlo felt better, safer.

From the time he heard about it as a kid playing on the streets, he had been intrigued by the Subs. Despite the cautionary stories from his parents and teachers, he made it his mission to know the downside. Getting access had not been easy for a young kid from a middle class family. After a few unpleasant early experiences, he had realized that the teachers were spies for the authorities and could and would get him and his parents in trouble. Most of them were little better than diggers, listening to the kids talk about their parents, for tidbits to reveal to the authorities.

His parents explained that spying was actually mandatory, that teachers with nothing to report would themselves be viewed with suspicion. Everyone who worked for the authorities were the same, his parents added. They were underpaid and unappreciated. Care must be taken whenever one dealt with a public servant. It was not unheard of for dentists to sneak truth serum into the anesthetic they used in order to release the inhibitions of patients and discover their secrets.

Arlo doubted this story. He had never personally known anyone who had a similar experience, but it was part of common folklore.

Finally, when Arlo was twelve, he was recruited for

a team created for kids who were not athletic. The C.E. had decided that everyone should have physical exercise so kids that were not in school teams were forced into sports regardless of their interest or aptitude. The remedial league from Arlo's school played remedial teams from other schools, and it was at one of these games Arlo met Diaz Trumbo. A big, beefy, slow-moving girl, Diaz had drawn the short straw for mandatory participation in sport. Diaz was even slower than Arlo, who was acknowledged the slowest runner on his team. On the day Arlo met Diaz, neither was playing or likely to be substituted and Arlo was attracted to Diaz because of her demeanor—she looked bored. He ambled over to say hello and saw that she was crying. Her slow running had begun to bother her. The other kids made fun of her because they were actually improving with practice while she was not.

Arlo commiserated with her and shared his opinion that like most of the things connected with school, athletics were a waste of time. Small and wiry, Arlo was actually getting better at sports, but he was just waiting to graduate so he could go to college where he could actually do something interesting. Diaz was a little wary at first, thinking he might be a provocateur, but she decided he was too outspoken. They started spending time together, first at league matches, then meeting after school. Diaz showed Arlo some of her personal work, actual drawings made by hand that she could not display at school. One day Arlo confided his fascination with the Subs. Diaz astounded him by saying, "I wish you had said something earlier. I know how to get into the Subs."

Arlo had been gobsmacked. Then he was skeptical.

As Diaz explained her knowledge, he was more and more excited. He wanted to go then, right at that very moment, but Diaz had demurred. Getting into the Subs was easy for her, but she knew he would want to stay and explore. She also knew they could not tell either of their parents or, for that matter, anyone else.

Diaz had found an access point to the Subs by accident when she was hiding from her brothers in the basement of her apartment building. Their parents had told them dire stories about what would happen if they went into the basement. It was where the building manager lived, a bad-tempered, bad-smelling old woman, with too few teeth. Her apartment was in the front of the building, lit by two dirty basement windows. Once in a while, the kids would try to peek through the windows—it was said she actually let a cat live in her space—but they never saw either or an animal. Although she was the manager, none of the tenants saw her do any work. As long as the heat and cooling were reliable, she was left in peace. The rest of the basement was a huge space filled with storage cages and junk.

Diaz's parents probably tried to scare the kids away from the basement from their natural parents' sense that kids will get into trouble if left to their own devices in empty spaces and abandoned structures of any kind. Although neither empty nor abandoned, the basement had a cautionary derelict feel that would entice any child and worry any parent.

Diaz's brothers were rambunctious twins with little respect for their big sister, who was fat and slow moving and interested only in protein shakes and drawing pictures. They refused to leave her things alone, and her parents were lackadaisical about punishing them. They found the twins more delightful than Diaz, who was dour and unattractive.

She took to exploring the basement. At first it was an accident; when she discovered that the stairwell door was unlocked, she was frightened of the dim place. As she tentatively descended and nothing terrible happened to her, she began to explore more thoroughly. The stairwell opened onto the roof, but the roof was too filthy and exposed. The basement, on the other hand, had a lot of promise. Behind the locked storage cubicles was a large open space and a number of small empty cubicles, some with actual tables and chairs. Diaz knew this was a place she could go to work on her drawings out of sight of her brothers. They were afraid of the basement, perhaps with more imagination than her or just more trusting of their parents' judgment.

So Diaz had enjoyed a few months of peace in a little cubby she fashioned. Inevitably, however, one day she heard sounds. Whether her brothers or the building manager or someone entirely different, perhaps one of the bogeys her parents raised, she didn't know. Flustered she grabbed her notebook and opened the nearest door, one she thought was a storage closet with only an ancient bucket and mop. There was a kind of curtain across the back encrusted with the filth of the ages. She had never wanted to touch it, but now she ducked behind it and found another door. The door was hard to see, fitted flush to the wall and painted the same color. She pushed on it tentatively, and it opened silently. Outside the storage closet, voices she now recognized as her brothers were running and screaming, opening doors and throwing chairs around. Eventually she knew they might open the storage room door and possibly look behind the filthy curtain. Dirt bothered them less than it did her.

Diaz pushed the hidden door open and ducked through into a long hallway lit by dim ceiling fixtures stretching forward as far as she could see. She closed the door behind her, sorry there was no lock, and jammed a pencil into the crack to make it hard to open.

She stood for a while, indecisive, trying to puzzle out where she was. At first she assumed she was in the basement of another apartment building, but the space looked different. The hallway was too long, the floor was covered with a kind of carpet so her footsteps were silent. In fact, the space was uncannily silent. She felt drawn to discover what was at the other end of the hallway.

Diaz stood for a long time when she finally arrived at the end of the hallway, looking at the door. Eventually she pushed it open to emerge into a huge open cave like space built of uneven blocks. A corridor went off to one side, and she could see other corridors opening off the opposite side of the space.

At that moment, an elderly man emerged from one of the tunnels and looked at her in surprise.

"Hello, girlie," he said. "Where did you spring from?"

She turned and pointed to the door behind her. "Where am I?" she asked.

The old man grinned. "What's you name, girlie?"

She told him, wondering if she should.

"Well, Diaz Trumbo," he said. "Welcome to the Subs."

Arlo was entranced when Diaz told him her story.

He wanted to leave immediately. He was ready to rush to the door in the basement of her apartment building and begin exploring. That door, Diaz said, was now locked and the corridor full of rubble as the result of one of the seismic events that happened periodically. The bedrock of the city seemed to be more active than seemed imaginable for a vast metropolis, and upheavals below occurred naturally and as result of construction above.

Now she had other points of access.

The Subs, as its name implied, were beneath the city and beneath the bedrock upon which the city was built. Its existence took advantage of natural fissures in the rock and tunnels built during the subway boom before the New Dispensation.

Diaz had insisted on waiting until her parents were away for a few days before venturing downside with Arlo. By now Diaz was in her late teens and could come and go at will, but her parents still cross-questioned her about her activities, and she hated to lie to them. Better to let them go out of the city for a few days.

When the time came, Diaz instructed Arlo to meet her in the toilet of a large public bathhouse downtown. No one paid attention to them as they moved among the constant flow of citizens relieving themselves, taking drugs, and having sex in the stalls. Diaz had directed Arlo to find a specific stall, then enter and pull down on the coat hook for a specific number of seconds. When he did so, a small door soundlessly opened and he went through, jubilant at finally being downside.

Diaz was waiting for him on a small ledge that led downward. The Subs appeared to be carved from stone, and as they walked, Diaz filled him in on some of the intricacies of negotiating through the tunnels.

Communication between the levels was difficult but not impossible, and Diaz had alerted one of her downside friends that she would be bringing a newcomer. The full-time residents of the Subs liked to keep newcomers to a minimum, and visitors who had found their way there were discouraged from bringing others.

Arlo followed Diaz to a small dwelling that had been a mobile home. He was introduced to her friends Father Maxwell and his nephew Piet Lem, both of whom would profoundly influence Arlo.

Father Maxwell was a priest of Isis/Osiris, the first religious Arlo had met, and he took to the older man immediately. Father M's nephew, Piet Lem, was a few years older than Arlo and had grown up in the Subs, although he had traveled extensively upside as part of his education.

When Arlo met him, he was reading an actual book, seemingly oblivious to the deadly virus hidden in the paper. Arlo looked at it aghast, and the young man laughed. "Don't worry. It won't kill you. The paper virus doesn't exist. It was just an excuse to destroy all the books. I've been reading them for years, and I'm still alive."

This was just the first of many shocking ideas that Arlo had encountered downside. Before he could do more exploring, he was closely examined by Father M and Piet Lem about his reasons for being there. Like many obsessions, it was difficult for Arlo to explain. Father M pointed out that most people upside believed the Subs was a myth or a metaphor for the sphere of criminal activity. Arlo could not explain why he had not believed in the myth. Somehow he tried to explain. He just knew that the Subs was real and that he had to see it for himself.

Diaz had listened for a while, then excused herself to visit another friend, an artist she had met who was showing her how to draw on paper. Arlo had been impressed with the difference in Diaz's behavior, by her confidence and air of competence. Upside she seemed taciturn and almost uncouth, unlovely physically, and mentally dull.

As he headed toward the Subs, Arlo realized he had not seen or talked with Diaz in a long time and felt some sadness. Father M had passed on a few years previously, but he thought he would ask Piet if he knew her whereabouts.

Piet Lem was still living in his uncle's trailer. Arlo found him having a beer and a sandwich. As he helped himself to a beer out of the cooler, Piet Lem said, "I'm trying to get some anti-inebriation drugs out of my system. Any ideas?"

Arlo had none. The drugs were very useful sometimes but lasted too long once they were no longer needed.

"I have a lead on the Command," Arlo said, telling him about Cosmo's conversation with Remy and the bartender at the club. "Irene Thorne," Piet Lem said musingly. "I think I've heard that name before." He then shared with Arlo his conversation with a drunken Jonson.

"Jonson says his customers are disappearing and the authorities are not doing anything. These customers must be from the upper reaches of society in order to have the money to realize their fantasies, even if they are being fooled."

"They must be ruthless bastards, too, if they are willing to consider snuff mode," Arlo said.

"Exactly, rich and connected. So why would the authorities turn a blind eye to their disappearances?"

Piet shrugged. "And would the authorities even care if they found out they were using unsanctioned sex workers? They don't usually worry much about homeless kids or off-the-books sex workers."

"Only if the Conclave is on the rampage about something and nothing has been coming out of there recently. In fact, there have been no news bulletins or edicts in a long time."

Arlo swigged his beer and said, "If they wanted these people disappeared, they would be gone."

Piet shook his head. "Yes, but they could just call the authorities and tell them, so-and-so has been deemed unsanctioned and the next day so-and-so is gone. A little note appears on the newscast and that's it."

"Those are usually citizens who have something the C.E. want, like guys who build an office building or who talk too much. These people are just rich pervos, and the C.E. usually don't seem to care about that sort of thing."

"Maybe they had something else in common," Piet Lem said.

"All I know is, Ana and Colt are not secret pervos and the Command seems to want to take them down. But they are not just disappearing them because that would be easy to do. Neither of them are hard to find. Ana is at the university most of the time, and Colt is out and around. Because of his gaming, his disappearance might not be surprising. People would think it was a gambling issue."

"But your friend Ana is a scientist. Her disappearance would cause talk. She doesn't have any obvious bad habits, like gambling or unsanctioned sex."

Arlo said very thoughtfully, unsure how to articulate his ideas, "I think Ana might be the target rather than Colt. There are troubling issues arising out at the university, or more properly, out at the Institute for Temporal Epistemology. Dr. Desmond Elvistine's institute," he amended, seeing Piet Lem's questioning look.

"Desmond Elvistine is probably the greatest mathematician of this or any century. He has already discovered and developed the protocol for opening the portal to an alternative universe."

Piet Lem said, "I thought that was a rumor. It was all over the news a couple of years ago, then it disappeared. I heard it was a fluke, the experiment could not be replicated."

"It was no fluke," Arlo said. "They opened a portal they cannot close, and the only person who has been able to decipher their communications is Dr. Ana Bede. I heard even Elvistine was not able to do it."

"So?" Piet Lem said.

"So maybe someone wants to break the link before any more communications are received."

"People were unhappy about the portal. They seemed to think the scientists had some role in creating the alternate universe." Piet Lem said thoughtfully. "It doesn't make sense to me. But as a resident of the Subs, I don't think like the citizens. Ideas are like magic for them."

"We can speculate all day, but I want to know who

Irene Thorne is and what she has to do with this group, if it exists. Who are they and what do they want? Are they actually disappearing people, or is the C.E. using them for secret missions."

Piet Lem promised he would talk to a few of the Grupo members and see what he could find out."

11

Teegan was leaving the apartment to carry their dirty clothes down to the basement through the stairwell when she realized she had forgot to pick up Jordi's favorite shirt from where he had thrown it behind the bedroom door. Cursing silently, she had backed out of the stairwell just in time to see a stranger coming up the stairs. Keeping the door cracked, she watched him pass her on the landing as he climbed upward. Leaving her laundry basket in the hall, she hurried to the elevator and pushed the button for the top floor.

When the elevator, slow at the best of times, finally reached the top, no one was in sight. She stepped carefully out of the elevator, prepared to pretend she had hit the wrong button, then followed the hallway around the perimeter of the building and up the stairs to the roof. The stranger was not on the roof; she climbed up to Ana's little platform to check there, but it was also empty.

Remaining alert, she walked down the stairs to the

apartment and looked through all the rooms. She decided that the business with Arlo and the dead digger had made her more paranoid than usual.

Feeling somewhat reassured, she picked up her basket and continued walking down to the basement where the cleaning unit was located. On the way she began to rationalize that all the tenants used the stairways rather than the elevator whenever possible. Usually they walked down rather than up, but the stranger was in good shape. Maybe he needed the exercise. He could have recently rented an apartment. The building was half empty; they were always looking for new tenants.

She tried to remember what the guy had looked like, but all she could remember was the silver ball hanging from the end of his pigtail. For the rest, he was wearing the same dark colors as every other citizen and seemed young, somewhere around her age. He had moved lightly, without touching the railing.

The attendant at the cleaning unit was named either Nadia or Irma. Teegan could not remember which, but it didn't seem to matter since the girl never seemed interested in small talk. Her job was to do the cleaning, using the cleaning mist machine, which had replaced units that used water. The machine was supposed to be too dangerous for untrained people to operate. Teegan doubted that piece of wisdom since Nadia or Irma seemed pretty stupid. Still she was happy to have her stuff taken care of and delivered to her door neatly folded.

Recognizing Teegan, the attendant slid a receipt disc toward her with a nod when Teegan put the basket on the counter.

"By the way," Teegan said, "are there any new tenants in the building? I thought I saw someone in the stairwell I didn't recognize."

"You know all the people in the building?" the attendant said.

"I try to. I've been here five years. I don't want any unsanctioned in the building."

The attendant looked affronted. Teegan noticed her name tag read Irma, but knew she would not remember it. "No one in the building is unsanctioned. Yet." she added.

"What do you mean by that?"

"People have been asking questions about your roommates, the professor and her husband."

Teegan felt all the symptoms of shock at once.

"People?" She kept her voice even.

"People. I didn't tell them anything. Management doesn't want me gossiping about the tenants. Besides they didn't offer anything for my efforts."

"Tell me about these people," Teegan said, feeling in her pocket for a cash token.

The attendant seemed uninterested. "There were two women, about your age. One was well dressed, nice clothes. She did all the talking. The other one looked like she just got into town, old clothes, stocking cap. She kept her mouth shut most of the time. It was maybe a week ago. They asked questions about Dr. Bede and her husband."

"What kind of questions?"

"Their apartment number, did they go out a lot, did they seem to have any money problems, pay their rent on time, that kind of thing." The attendant also collected rent from those who paid it.

"They asked about you and your husband, too."

Teegan could see Irma was enjoying her discomfort. "Same kind of questions, but they wanted to know if you were fooling around with Mr. Bede and vice versa."

"What a crazy question. What did you say?"

Irma leaned forward, confidingly. "I said, 'Not that I knew of. I don't spy on the tenants.' Then one of them said, 'Oh, we know you wouldn't do something like that, but you know what goes on in the building. It's your responsibility, and we're sure you are interested in people.' They were trying to be friendly, casual. They were creepy or I might have told them something."

"What something" Teegan said sharply.

Affronted, Irma said, "Oh, I don't know, something about Mr. Bede being a gambler. Something like that. But as I say, they were creepy and didn't offer me anything for my trouble so I just said I didn't know much about them. I said they should go to the university where Dr. Bede works and ask questions there. Then the dumpy one said something like, *we tried that, they wouldn't talk to us,* and the other one gave her a dirty look."

"And you're sure there are no new tenants in the building? Have you seen a young guy with a long braid with a ball hanging on it?"

"You mean a fighting ball. Like a martial artist?"

"I guess that's what it is. I just thought it was an ornament."

"They are used for fighting, and I haven't seen anyone like that."

Teegan slid two cash tokens over to the girl.

"Here, Irma. For your trouble. Let one of us know if the women or anyone else come to ask questions.

Okay?"

Looking happier, Irma took the tokens and turned back to the cleaning machine.

When Teegan returned to the apartment, Colt and Jordi had arrive and she told them about seeing the stranger in the stairwell. When she described the ball hanging from his braid. Colt said, "Say that again," obviously upset.

Teegan said, "The only thing I remember about him is that he had a long braid with a ball swinging from it. The building attendant said it was a fighting ball."

"Damn," Colt said. "Chandler Besdine."

"Who?" Teegan and Jordi said together.

"Chandler Besdine was in Ana's advanced math series taught by Dr. Elvistine and another professor named Tillman."

"I remember Tillman," Teegan said. "He got into some kind of trouble with the authorities."

Colt ignored her. "Do you remember me telling you about a guy I played MJ with who followed me and made comments about Elvistine?"

"And he, *quote,* borrowed, *unquote,* some cash from you." Jordi said.

"That's him. Today I went to the university to see Ana, and Elvistine got all excited when I mentioned Chandler. He blew up about Tillman and planned to rush off to see his contact in the Conclave of Elders. He wanted Ana to go but I told her not to. I don't want Ana near the Conclave or any of their representatives."

"What's the deal with this Tillman?" Teegan asked.

"I wish I knew. I don't understand this stuff. I

think Tillman was doing some kind of competing research."

Colt jumped up and started doing snippets of martial arts katas, something he did when he was tense.

"So you looked around for this guy and couldn't find him?"

Teegan told them about her conversation with the building attendant, about the two women who were inquiring about Colt and Ana. The attendant's descriptions of the women were vague, but it was clear from her account that the women were not from the authorities. No one around the table thought their appearance and the appearance of the stranger, presumably Chandler Besdine, were coincidental.

Colt walked her through the timing of the stranger's appearance, trying to determine how long he had been in the building, whether he had time to get into their apartment.

"How hard would it be to get past the lock?" Teegan wanted to know.

"Probably not hard if you have the right equipment," Colt said.

"If he did get into the apartment, he was in and out in a very short time. There's not much here to steal and Ana keeps anything connected with her work at the university."

"Maybe he planted a listening device," Jordi suggested. "If he did, he knows Teegan saw him and that we know he's interested in Colt and Ana." They all looked at each other, reluctant to say anything further.

Colt stopped doing katas and cracked his knuckles, a loud sound in the suddenly quiet room.

He picked up his backpack where he had thrown it on the floor, flipped it over his shoulder, and stalked out.

After he had gone, Jordi and Teegan stood awkwardly in the living room, suddenly unwilling to say anything. Finally, Jordi headed for their bedroom, and Teegan followed. He grabbed a shoulder bag and took a few more cash tokens than he usually carried. Teegan watched him curiously as he picked up her leather jacket and tossed it to her, then headed for the door.

From her position across the street from their apartment building, Linnet watched them emerge. Colt had come out earlier and headed uptown, toward the entertainment district. Teegan and Jordi headed in that direction also and she followed along, keeping well back. Her task was easy because the streets were busy.

She was torn by what she was doing, not so much following Teegan and Jordi, whom she did not know, but following Colt, who had done so much for her. Irene had explained how essential her reporting was, how they needed to know what Colt and Ana were doing every minute, that at any moment they could do something that would destroy the city. When Linnet had tried to determine what they could do, she envisioned a powerful bomb or even another plague. Irene had held her face between her hands so that Linnet had to stare into those mesmerizing eyes and said, "This is worse, much worse than the plague. This could destroy everything."

"Why weren't the authorities acting," Linnet had asked. "If they were so dangerous, why is this small group of citizens taking responsibility?"

"The authorities," Irene had said bitterly, "are fools and do not understand what can happen if Elvistine is permitted to continue. It is up to us, darling. We are citizen warriors." Linnet knew Irene was a rich, beautiful, connected citizen who, for some reason, cared for Linnet passionately. If she wanted Linnet to be a citizen warrior, that's how it would be.

12

Linnet's training at the House of Blue Leaves had included instruction in the four modes of pleasure, one of which was sex with people of one's own gender. As far as Linnet knew, this concept did not exist at home in Heartsease, and the possibility had never occurred to her independently. Amused, Sparrow, the manager of the house, had explained that this was a sanctioned activity and enlisted the help of the other girls to train Linnet.

In the community where Linnet had lived, the sexes had been strictly segregated until they were partnered when the girls reached puberty. The actual mechanics of partnering had not been discussed, and both genders were strictly forbidden any contact outside sanctioned marriage.

Linnet, for her part, never discussed sex with the other girls. She had few close friends; her two older and two younger sisters naturally gravitated to each other, but Linnet, the middle child, was left alone.

Her mother was always busy in the communal kitchen. Aside from a weekly dinner with her father, she never saw him, and he paid little attention to her.

School left Linnet as lonely as family life. Perhaps she was a natural outsider or perhaps because of her father's high status, the other girls did not seek her out. Quiet obedience was a valued behavior in the community, and Linnet found the ability to efface herself invaluable. No one cared what she, or any of the girls, was thinking.

However, from an early age, Linnet had been interested in life outside the community. Her early questions were lovingly rebuffed, but as she grew older such questions were met with anger and fear. The one brother she had a close relationship with took her aside and explained that asking questions was unsafe and would lead to attention from the community elders. Attention from the patriarchs was never a good thing. Even positive attention was avoided if at all possible.

Linnet had been pleasantly surprised to find when she was partnered with Oren that he was also interested in the outside world. Oren was simple enough to lack the ability to self-censor, and, like Linnet, he had a lonely childhood, being neither athletic nor intellectually skilled. His powers of observation were acute, however, and he had noticed and discovered quite a number of interesting activities carried on by the community patriarchs that he shared with her and that eventually enabled her to leave.

Although she was glad to find herself in the city and, after the first rough couple of weeks, to be taken in by Colt and Mauritz. But she had still found herself lonely.

After the first shock, work at the House was easy and predictable. Sparrow ensured that the sex workers were protected from violence and reasonably well paid. During down times, the boys and girls would talk about things Linnet knew nothing about styles, videos, dating, moving into society. Many of them wanted to open shops of their own since, except for some of the specialized houses, sex work was for youngsters. For Linnet, everything was puzzling and dull.

Back in her room, Linnet found herself watching kids' vids, then wandering the streets when she could not sleep.

Irene had completely transformed her boring, rather sad, life. Linnet thought that, if other, more experienced girls had been available, Linnet would not have been assigned to Irene. It was well known that Linnet was not very good at sex with women. No actual complaints had been recorded, but clients had suggested that she might need more training or, one said, "an enthusiasm injection."

One busy night, Linnet found herself in a studio with a beautiful nude blond woman lounging in the client's chair. Her startling blue eyes almost glittered in the low light, and she spoke in a deep masculine voice. Linnet had assumed the customer was trans-gendered, but she was wrong.

Linnet had stood nervously twisting her hair, and Irene had immediately taken charge of the situation, hopping out of the chair and laughing, telling her to relax, asking her name, seating her in front of one of the big mirrors that were sanctioned for the House, the C.E. apparently not concerned with soul loss in a brothel.

Feeling ugly and clumsy, Linnet watched in the mirror as the older woman picked up a brush and started to brush her hair which fell to her waist.

"It's unusual to see hair this long," she said. "When did you have it cut last?"

"I, I cut it myself," Linnet said, "on Elders' Day. It's the custom where I come from."

Irene held up a lock of hair. "What did you use? Hedge clippers?"

"I used scissors," Linnet said seriously.

"Well, we can fix this," Irene said. Linnet wondered when they had become "we."

She put the brush down. "But it's better now. It was full of rats' nests."

Linnet jumped, looked with horror-stricken eyes at Irene. "No, I washed it," she said.

Irene laughed again. "That's just a very old expression for tangles, darling."

Darling? What did that mean?

Irene leaned forward and wrapped Linnet's hair around her arm in a complicated gesture that pulled Linnet's head back then lowered her own head to gently kiss the bare skin of her neck.

Linnet was now frankly terrified. She could act out the modes of pleasure satisfactorily if there was no personal gestures like this kiss on the neck. Linnet's new friend Soliel, who had appointed herself Linnet's mentor, said she was getting better at them. "You almost seem to enjoy yourself," she had laughed. Now Linnet feared she had lost control of the encounter.

"You're new at this, aren't you?" Irene whispered in her ear.

"Yes."

"Do you like sex with women?"

"Oh, yes." Linnet was sure of this answer. Whatever the client wanted to do, as long as it was within the appropriate mode of pleasure, was liked by the employee.

Irene laughed. "I'll bet you've never had an orgasm with a woman."

"Oh, no, I have," Linnet assured her. "My friend Soliel showed me how to do everything. I've got my level one certificate."

"And you enjoyed yourself with your friend Soliel?"

"Oh, yes." Linnet was enthusiastic now. "Soliel is working on her level two certificate. She plans to go into private service after that. She's very pretty," Linnet added, to assure Irene that Soliel would be successful in private service. Private service meant you were still affiliated and protected by the house, but you went to the client. It was slightly more dangerous, but paid very well.

Irene was clearly enjoying herself. "I think you need a glass of wine," she said, standing up, which pulled Linnet to her feet also. Irene didn't release her hair, rather used it to lead her over to the client's chair.

"Sit here," she said, pushing Linnet into the seat.

"Oh, no. You're supposed to sit here," Linnet said.

"Isn't the client always right?" Irene spoke into the intercom, asking for a bottle of champagne and two glasses. She looked at Linnet, reclining stiffly in the chair. "You're a little thin, darling. Would you like something to eat?"

All Linnet could do was shake her head. Champagne? All the boys and girls talked about it, but few workers sanctioned at the basic level had ever tasted it. Beginning to feel a small flicker of excitement, Linnet looked around the room from the comfort of the client's chair, a complicated piece of furniture that was part chair, part bed, part chaise longue. It was extremely comfortable and did a lot of tricks designed to maximize access to all the salient body parts.

While waiting for the champagne, Irene had gone over to the mirror and was fiddling with her hair. She was a tall muscular woman, sleek. Her skin was exceptionally smooth. The House of Blue Leaves catered to older citizens, but Irene was not one of their usual clientele. Linnet thought she must be just a few years older than herself. Her hands were beautiful, and she moved with self-confidence rare among citizens who lived, if not in fear, at least in caution.

The door made a melodious sound, and at Irene's voice command, a hatch slid up revealing an open champagne bottle and two fragile-looking glasses. Linnet made a feeble effort to stand up. She should be doing to serving, she thought, but Irene just pushed her back into the chair and picked up the tray, placing it on a low table in handy reach of the couch, and seated herself next to Linnet's legs.

She poured out two glasses of bubbly liquid and handed one to Linnet, commanding her to sip it slowly.

It tasted good, cool and effervescent. Linnet took another sip. She felt herself unwind a little. Maybe this would not be too bad. This woman seemed nice; she was beautiful and rich. She knew Linnet was certified at the lowest levels. Linnet felt a momentary qualm; maybe drinking champagne was not part of the basic levels. Maybe that's why she had never had any. Maybe she was only certified for cheap wine. She took another sip. She didn't care, she decided.

The woman had been watching her closely as she sipped, watching the worry incrementally smooth out of her face. The girl was really thin; her hands showed no care but a history of work; her hair was a mess. She had a pretty good idea of the girl's background, either in the Subs or possibly a runaway from another city or some communal enclave in the countryside. She liked that. It showed determination and resilience—and vulnerability.

Irene said a word, and music began to play somewhere in the background. She took the glass of wine gently from the girl's hand, setting it on the table, and then kicking the table away with her foot. A hand gesture and the lights dimmed. The girl stirred a little, but the older woman leaned forward and ran a finger from the notch of her throat, past her breasts, and over her stomach, stopping just below her navel.

Reaching down, she opened a drawer set into the base of the chair and pulled out a small cylindrical object, which she laid on the table, followed by some other items Linnet could not see.

Irene reached over and patted her on the cheek, picking up the object, which vibrated gently.

"Let's start with this," she had said.

13

Colt was of two minds whether to return to the institute or to search for Arlo, who, Colt felt, might know what was going on. Colt's feelings about Arlo were decidedly mixed. In college they had been very close, and Colt could not find it in his heart to blame Arlo for caring for Ana. He did himself; she was the world to him.

He could admit to himself that he no longer knew whether she felt that way about him. And Linnet was a complicating factor. He was concerned about her. She seemed so vulnerable in the city after growing up in some obscure little commune. Teegan had been raised in a communal marriage—it was pretty common in the N.D.—but her upbringing had not been as strict as Linnet's. Teegan was tough. Colt worried about Linnet, had tried to think about a way to bring her into the circle with Ana, Teegan, and Jordi; a circle of protection.

Even though she was never far from his thoughts,

he had not seen her in several weeks except for brief moments when he had stopped by the House of Blue Leaves. She had seemed to be fitting in and making friends with some of the kids. A girl named Soliel had taken Linnet under her wing.

He decided he had more important things to do than worry about Linnet. She was safe with Sparrow. Finding Arlo was more important, and finding him should be no problem. Colt had spent time in the Subs. They didn't call to him like they did to Arlo, but he enjoyed the feeling of freedom being there. He had liked Piet Lem, too. From what Arlo had confided, Grupo did good work looking after the citizens who had to seek sanctuary for one reason or another beneath the city.

Colt had been walking steadily away from the apartment building, generally in the direction of the university and the entertainment district. The easiest way downside was through Sandy's basement. Teegan and Jordi would go to Sandy's at some point and he could leave a message for them with Leland.

Like most clubs, Sandy's was open 24/7, and now in the late afternoon, daylight was almost completely gone and the early evening crowds were gathering. Sandy's was still not very busy, a few tables filled, and Leland was half watching a video screen under the bar. When Colt took a seat at the bar, Leland automatically brought him a bourbon.

"Hello Colt. We haven't see you in a long time. Is the goddess of luck smiling upon you?"

"So-so." Colt drank the bourbon, but shook his head when Leland reached for the bottle. "Have you seen any more of Arlo?"

Leland leaned confidentially across the bar. "No,

but someone was in here asking about you. A day or two ago, a woman came in, young, well dressed, unhappy looking, dark hair. She looked like she might be a college student. She had several drinks, then asked me if I knew someone named Colt Bede. I said a guy named Colt came into the bar sometimes, but that was all I knew. I asked her to describe the guy she was looking for, and she did a pretty good job of describing you. What do you want him for, I asked. She said she just wanted to talk with you about a mutual friend."

"Did she tell you the name of the mutual friend?"

"If she did, it was not a name I recognized. At first I thought she might be a new girlfriend, but Teegan and Jordi came in while she was here, and she didn't seem to recognize them. It occurred to me you might owe some people money, having a bad run of MJ, but she didn't look the type."

Sandy's consisted of a long room with an old fashioned bar almost the entire length. Later in the evening, another bartender would come in and help Leland, and if needed, the cook could step in. There was no table service.

Colt had drifted to the back of the room where he could watch who came in and then duck into the basement for his visit downside. Teegan and Jordi came in then, waving as they spotted him. Behind them in the street light, Colt thought he saw Linnet. The sight surprised him. He thought she would be working.

Teegan sat down beside him, and Leland put a vodka in front of her. Jordi didn't sit, but fist-bumped with Colt in greeting.

"I'm going down the street for a sandwich. You

want me to bring you anything" he said.

Colt demurred, but Teegan gave him her order, and he headed down the length of the club and through the door. Colt watched him casually as he left, still thinking about the mysterious citizens who were suddenly interested in Ana and himself. Linnet had apparently been hanging around outside the club because when Jordi turned left, she appeared to be following him.

It was a crazy idea. As far as Colt knew, Linnet didn't know Jordi.

Leland had moved down the bar, leaving Colt to sit in silence with Teegan. When he judged Jordi would be coming back from the sandwich shop, he ducked out the back door into the alley and positioned himself so he could see the sidewalk without being seen. Jordi approached shortly, a sandwich bag in his hand, and across the street, Colt saw Linnet, obviously following. When Jordi went into the club, Linnet took up a position in the shadows.

He thought about approaching her, finding out what she was doing watching his friends. Before he could do so, a taxi pulled up outside the door to the bar, and when it discharged its passengers and drove away, Linnet was gone. He thought briefly about his priorities and decided to find Arlo. Linnet could wait.

Back inside, Colt grabbed his backpack and stood between Teegan and Jordi, arms around both of them.

"You are being followed," he said. "I am going to find Arlo and try to find out what is going on. I think Ana and I are the targets of all this, but I don't want you to get hurt. If I can get you travel passes out of the city, is there some place you could go? Maybe visit Teegan's family."

Teegan grimaced. "We hate the countryside. It's more dangerous than the Subs. We're staying in the city."

Jordi looked at Teegan hopefully, "We could go visit Rick and Ilsa. They live on the coast in Deep Cove, and Rick would love to see us. Now that Ilsa finally moved in with him, he's bored.

"Go," Teegan said. "I'm staying here. I can't afford to just drop my job and go to the country."

Colt shrugged. "Whatever you decide, be careful. I think Ana and I are the objects of these people, whoever they are. I think it has something to do with Ana's work at the institute. I don't want you guys to be swept up in it." He kissed Teegan on the cheek and fist-bumped Jordi once more.

Colt found Arlo by the simple expedient of finding Piet Lem, the chieftain of Grupo Uno and the de facto ruler of the Subs. The two men were sitting with a third at a table holding a samovar and tea paraphernalia. All three men pushed their chairs away from the table as Colt tossed his backpack on the ground. Piet fist bumped Colt and said, "Colt, I expected you."

Colt crossed his arms and stared at Arlo. "What's going on?"

Arlo smiled slightly. "That's the question."

Piet Lem put another cup on the table, put a cube of sugar in it and poured tea from the teapot. He nodded toward an empty chair and said, "We were just getting a report from our friend Belasco about a citizen named Irene Thorne, who seems to be at the center of all this."

Belasco nodded gracefully. He looked out of place in the Subs. His pants and tunic in matching muted shades of dark gray were custom-made, and he wore a simple signet ring that set him apart as a member of the privileged classes. The suit's beautiful trousers were cuffed over leather boots. A sumptuous leather messenger bag hung from the back of his chair. Colt noted that, for all his apparent upside sophistication, he seemed unaffected by the atmosphere of the Subs.

When he spoke, his tones were equally polished. "Irene Thorne is the daughter of an industrialist who had close ties to the Conclave of Elders. His name was Chrismundo Trelawney. You may have heard of him. Irene took her mother's name, like many women in her class, out of respect, she said. Her father was a chemical engineer and inventor who used his knowledge to develop several highly successful processes for growing the synthetic petroleum which is now used for power when nuclear generation is too expensive. He had extensive holdings in algae farms and petroleum manufacturing plants and in nuclear generators. He had several wives and partners, never settling for one very long, and numerous offspring. Irene's mother died in Irene's early teens, but she never lived with her mother. Irene was Chrismundo's eldest and, by all accounts, most intelligent child. They were very close."

Belasco added as an aside, "It's strange that she later became so anti-science and suspicious of scientific inquiry because her father was a famous scientist."

He then continued, "Unlike his other children, who were sent to sanctioned boarding schools in the countryside, Irene's father educated her at an academy in the city where her work was brilliant and her reputation questionable. Although gossiping about someone with her father's connections was dangerous, numerous of her schoolmates describe her as cold, vindictive, and, a word that was often used among people I talked with, crazy. After secondary school, she went to law school, where she excelled, specializing in commerce and business. When she became a sanctioned lawyer, she went to work for a small, powerful lobbying firm. She quickly became a partner, then senior partner. Citizens with whom she had problems—partners in the firm and their families, for example—experienced unfortunate accidents. People were, quite frankly, scared to death of her.

"She continued to live at home while her personal life revolved around a series of intense relationships with people of either gender. Most of the people I talked with thought she preferred women, but no one wanted to get close enough to her to find out.

"People in her close circle would occasionally just vanish."

Belasco paused and sipped his tea. "I do not know her personally. All that I am telling you is second hand. I have met her at large social events, but that is as close as I want to get to her. I will say that she is a beautiful woman, intensely charismatic.

"To continue, a couple of years ago, her father died very suddenly. His heart stopped. The healers attributed it to an infarct and claimed he could have been saved if he had been seen sooner. At the time, he was vacationing in the countryside at a spa with his most recent mistress. Irene was in the city.

"Of course there were rumors, but the authorities

did nothing, no surprise there," he laughed and so did the other three men.

"Irene seemed bereft. Rumor had it she had a fight with her father right before his death, but no one I talked with knew the substance. At any rate, with her father's death, she inherited a lot of money. No one knows how much, but her father had enough to go around for all his exes and children. The businesses went to the sons. No rumors have floated that any of the kids were disappointed.

"Then things got interesting. Irene resigned from her law firm and moved out of the family home into a modest apartment with two of her friends. No one knows these women or what their connection is with Irene. They are certainly not from her usual social circle.

"Lately—and I mean within the last two weeks—she has been spending a lot of time at a sex club called The House of Blue Leaves. The story is that she has become enamored of one of the sex workers, but my sources did not know who or even if it was true. Maybe she just wants to have a lot of sex all of a sudden."

Colt, who had been looking moodily at his teacup while Belasco told his story, looked up sharply at this mention of the House of Blue Leaves. The other men looked at him curiously. He told them about his rescue of Linnet from the streets and his discovery earlier in the evening that she was following his roommate.

"You think Irene found out about your connection with Linnet and decided to use her to spy on you? That seems far-fetched," Piet said.

"Everything about this matter seems far-fetched,"

Arlo put in. "I originally came back to the city because one of my contacts here told me that he had heard a very reliable rumor that someone was out to get Ana Bede. This friend knew of my feelings for Ana, and she thought Ana might be in trouble. I got in touch with Piet immediately, and we tried to find out where the rumor originated. For a long time we were unsuccessful, but we started hearing stories about a group called the Command."

Arlo continued, "finding out more about this group was difficult, but I finally connected with a digger named Cosmo Naftali, who recognized a woman who was supposed to be one of the group. She was pointed out to him in a club as a member of this group, and he knew her from elementary school. I had him find her and pretend to meet her by accident. And get this: she is one of Irene Thorne's roommates. Her name is Remy Clon, and she is certainly not from Chrismundo Trelawney's social circle."

He turned to Belasco. "What have you heard about the Command? Do you have any solid information?"

"Solid, no. They are supposed to be responsible for the disappearance of several citizens in the higher strata of society. There is no noticeable pattern to these disappearances, no connections among the victims, except that the authorities are not taking any action to find out what happened to these people. They take a report, interview the family or business associates, then the matter drops."

"We were told that several people with violent sexual habits had recently disappeared," Piet Lem said.

"Maybe they are the same people. A taste for extreme S&M is usually not common knowledge, but if the authorities became involved, they would probably take some kind of action. It would depend on who was harmed."

"Is Irene Thorne mentioned in connection with these disappearances?" Piet Lem asked.

"Not that I know of. Irene has always been rumored to get rid of people standing in her way to consolidating her power. I've never heard that she was involved with a political group of any kind.

"Participating in a groups is not her style. She is in charge, and everyone else is not. When she was working for the lobbying firm she had a materialist view. She was always trying to get the funding cut for any group that was primarily ephemerist oriented, like think tanks. At one point she tried to get funding cut for the planetarium on the grounds that research into black holes was ephemerist and therefore dangerous."

Piet said, "That might explain why she has it in for Ana. Ana's institute is on the cutting edge of ephemerist thought. Ana's compatriot, Dr. Desmond Elvistine, developed the protocol for communicating with alternate universes. Ana and Dr. Elvistine hate those materialist and ephemerist labels, but they are stuck with them."

Belasco smiled. "The work of the institute would definitely get Irene's knickers in a twist." He stood up and shouldered his beautiful leather bag. Colt tried unsuccessfully to imagine how much it cost.

Piet Lem also stood up and they had a brief manly hug, exchanging delighted noises; then Piet Lem walked Belasco to the entry of one of the tunnels.

When he returned, Colt said, "Who is he?"

Piet Lem laughed and put a bottle of cognac, shockingly rare and expensive, usually available only to the highest levels of society, on the table.

"A gift from Yonatan. He and I do some business occasionally. He sometimes has need of rare drugs that I can supply. He uses them in his profession as a sanctioned re-educator." He grinned at their shocked expressions. "Very few of them exist, but if you are highly enough placed, instead of going to a re-education facility, you can hire Yonatan, pay him a lot of money, and he'll restore your sanctioned status."

"He can do that?" Arlo asked.

"They say he is related to an elder."

"It would take that, at least," Colt said. "But why does he need drugs? He doesn't look like a druggie."

"He's not. He is strictly straight edge. He uses them in his work. After all, not everyone wants to be re-educated. They develop unsanctioned convictions. They are infected with wrong beliefs. Sometimes drug therapy is needed to bring the patient back to sanctioned thinking. Yonatan has found that the drugs he has available upside are not strong enough, safer though they may be, to do the job."

"I don't want to think about it," Arlo said.

The three men savored the rare and delicious cognac while deciding what steps to take. They needed still more information about Irene, and Colt was worried about Ana. Linnet seemed like a good lead; Colt wanted to talk to her immediately, but he wanted Ana out of the city. He decided it might be a good idea for her to go with Elvistine, who had passes, on his trip to see his contact at the Conclave. They decided that Arlo would try to contact Teegan and Jordi and, through them, Ana to urge her to go with Elvistine and drop out of sight for a while. Meanwhile Colt would try to find Linnet.

14

Colt exited the Subs into a subway tunnel that provided him a free trip to the entertainment district and the House of Blue Leaves. The entrance resembled a small residential hotel with a few dusty chairs and a desk clerk to collect the cover charge. Entrance to the club was via a rickety elevator at the back of the lobby. The walls were painted with blue and silver leaves and illuminated by small, twinkling silver lights. Sometimes, when business was slow, one of the employees would be draped over the counter in a provocative manner, but today only a woman named Trinity was taking cash tokens. Colt knew her from previous visits with Linnet and had found her pleasantly chatty. She recognized him when he entered, pushed a button under the desk that opened the door to the elevator, saying abruptly "You here for Linnet? See Sparrow."

Sparrow was waiting for Colt by the elevator. Plump and epicene, his usual welcoming smile was missing, and his fist-bump perfunctory.

They were standing in a large foyer with corridors branching in different directions and a cafe on the left. Several boys and girls sprawled suggestively on couches in the center.

"Colt, I am glad to see you. I was just going to have a meal. Join me in the café, and we will discuss Linnet."

"She's not here?" Colt frowned.

"Not at the moment." The cafe was surprisingly cozy with lighting that almost resembled daylight. Serious partying took place in a club upstairs.

Colt followed Sparrow to a table in the rear, facing the entrance. Without being asked, a waiter brought tea and bread. Sparrow asked if he wanted something stronger, but Colt, still a little buzzed from the cognac, opted for tea.

"I cannot decide whether I am more worried or more angry with Linnet," Sparrow said. "She has quit living in the residential hotel with Soliel and has taken a bed in the dormitory we keep for some of our employees, those who are freelance and just need a bed for a few days a month. Linnet is hardly ever there. She spends all her time with her new girlfriend, Irene. Do you know her?"

He didn't wait for a reply. "Linnet has almost entirely quit working. Admittedly she was not one of my best girls, but now she only takes quickies because she is waiting for Irene to come in or to summon her to her apartment. Of course, Irene pays me when she comes here, but not enough to compensate me for the loss of a full-time employee. I would fire her, but where would she go? If she quits, that's another story, but she hasn't quit. This Irene person has money. She was a prominent lawyer until she had a breakdown and dropped out of sight. She has a very bad reputation. I don't want to mess with her." Sparrow shook his head sadly as the waiter brought bowls of delicious looking pasta and small dishes of bitter greens.

"What's her problem?" Colt was interested in Sparrow's opinion. He had an extensive network of contacts in spheres different from Yonatan Belasco.

"This is all rumor. My clientele are sadly no longer those at the very top of society, but they are well placed and of old families, as much as those still exist. This Irene's father was very famous, very rich, an industrialist. He liked women, always had a wife or a mistress, but some of my acquaintances who cater to those citizens say he was essentially austere, even puritanical. For example, he never patronized sex workers, even though he had access to the most beautiful and gifted ones. Irene was his favorite child, and from the beginning, she was determined to get her way in everything. He would deny her nothing, and if her father's wealth and power could not accomplish what she wanted, she would resort to the Subs. People would get out of the way, one way or another." Sparrow waved a hand on which the ghosts of removed tattoos still lingered. "That's what I've heard."

"She had a breakdown, you said," Colt prodded.

Sparrow shrugged pudgy shoulders and thoughtfully ate some pasta. "Rumor has it that Irene and her father were arguing because Irene wanted to drop out of society and pursue some agenda—no one seems to know what it was—and her father wanted her to have children. She was the most brilliant of his children, and he thought her children would be more brilliant than both of them. Supposedly he had lined up some outstanding sperm donors for her if she was willing. He had vetted the surrogates, taken care of everything. All she had to do was contribute an egg or two."

"But she refused."

"She said she would only participate if her father got sperm from the most brilliant men in the world. She had a list. At the top of the list was a brilliant, deep scientist from the city."

Stunned, Colt forgot to chew. "She wanted Desmond Elvistine's sperm."

"Oh, yes. Her father was livid. Elvistine is the epitome of the deep scientist, the ephermerist's ephemerist, everything her father hated. I'm sure the sperm he had in mind came from the materialist camp."

"Would Elvistine even participate in such an activity, if that's what it is?"

"I don't know the citizen," Sparrow said.

"I do. Elvistine and my wife are colleagues in the university's Institute for Temporal Epistemology. Ana was his protégé. I've known him for a very long time. I don't know if he would contribute his sperm to make a superbaby?"

Colt ate some delicious pasta and thought about Elvistine, his obsession with his work. Colt could not remember his taking a vacation or going to a party, even the formal faculty parties that Ana insisted she and Colt attend. Sparrow said nothing.

"I don't know." Colt continued. "He isn't married, and I've never known him to show an interest in partnering. He's married to his work. Ana's the only woman he has spent any time with for the past ten years. And, trust me, their relationship is not personal. I don't know if he patronizes sex clubs such as this house."

"There are some very selective private clubs that require one to become a member, very discreet."

"I expect the dues are considerable," Colt said.

"Astronomical, but the services are comprehensive and delivered in the most opulent settings utilizing state-of-the-art technology. And membership is completely confidential." Colt thought Sparrow sounded wistful.

"I can't imagine Elvistine spending large money for sex. His funds all go to the institute. The research equipment is expensive, and he has to pay top salaries to keep staff."

"Such as your wife," Sparrow said.

"Especially my wife. She could go to any university in the world and be hired tomorrow, and Elvistine knows it." Colt wondered for the millionth time why she had married him.

"Would he contribute sperm if the payment was commensurate with his needs?" Sparrow asked. "How much does he value his own excellence? Would it be important for him to continue his genetic contributions?"

"All good questions I don't know the answers to. How do we know Irene is still pursuing Elvistine's sperm? Possibly she used him as a sock puppet to defuse her father's demands, knowing her father would never consider him an appropriate donor."

Sparrow waved a pudgy ring-encrusted hand. "None of these considerations address why she is pursuing our little Linnet, who has nothing to recommend her except beautiful hair. Those intentional communities in the countryside raise their kids in boxes; no piece of information gets to them that is not controlled by the community leaders. They are brought up to work and, if they are girls and fertile, to have babies. They sell all the produce of the community and keep everything. The managers get rich. You see them all the time at the big clubs when they come into the city on business.

"She escaped from her community. That took curiosity and courage," Colt said.

Sparrow smiled. "You know what they say about curiosity. God had curiosity when he created the world, and then it killed him.

"But here's the thing," Sparrow said, uncomfortably. "I blame myself. Linnet is fertile, apparently. She bleeds, and I had a standing offer from some clients, Irene Thorne among them, to advise them when I hired a girl who was surrogate material. Many people want to avoid professional surrogates."

Colt was outraged. "You told Irene that Linnet was fertile, for a price."

"I did not." Sparrow looked affronted. "Linnet is not a very bright young girl, not charming. I would act as her agent, arrange terms. But Irene Thorne came along, began to monopolize her. Linnet would not listen to me. Some of the other kids must have told Irene about her."

"I need to talk to Linnet." Colt finished his tea and stood up. Sparrow stood also and moved toward the foyer. He said, "We'll ask Roman and Soliel if they have any idea when she will return. They are her best friends among the kids."

Roman and Soliel had little information for them. They were both worried about Linnet, who seemed to them simultaneously obsessed with Irene and afraid of her.

"She doesn't say much," Soliel looked worried. "She says Irene is in love with her and wants to have sex with her all the time, but refuses to let her stay in the apartment and will not introduce Linnet to her roommates. She tells Linnet the roommates are not her lovers but part of a very important organization that Irene heads. But she won't tell Linnet anything about the organization. Poor kid. She's getting too much sex and not enough love."

They both promised to contact Sparrow immediately if Linnet contacted either of them or returned to the club, and Sparrow promised to contact Colt.

It was after midnight when Colt left the club. Business at the House of Blue Leaves was good; the elevator was slowly clattering down from the penthouse club so Colt took the stairs down to street level. He was becoming seriously worried about Ana. If she would not leave town, he planned to try to force her to take refuge with Piet Lem or one of Piet's pals in the Subs. All he had were rumors that Irene had contacts there and even if she did, he was confident Piet and his people could protect Ana. Piet would require money, but Ana had money. She saved most of her considerable salary, and she had numerous sanctioned credits, enough to pay for protection.

Either fortuitously or by design, the stairs from the house left one in a side street, away from the main entrance. Colt began heading for the lights of the street, then stopped to reconsider. Getting back to the apartment through less traveled back streets could take a little longer, but he would feel more secure. His military and martial arts training might finally provide some benefit if he was followed or attacked.

No one followed him or menaced him while he lurked through the night dark streets, stumbling across a few citizens doing the kinds of things one does in dark corners, and none happy to see him.

He entered the apartment building through the basement, stopping in at the attendant's office, but she was not at her counter. Although she lived in the building, Colt decided not to knock her up and made a mental note to see her in the morning.

Taking the stairs two at a time, he arrived at his floor breathless, realizing how tired he was.

The apartment was dark except for a light under Teegan and Jordi's door that opened immediately when they heard the outer door open.

Colt flicked on the light, and Teegan and Jordi, both dressed for the outdoors, both looking worried, pointed to two full backpacks on the couch. Teegan then pointed to a fitting for an old-fashioned light fixture, no longer used, that protruded through the ceiling. Then she pointed to her ear, indicating that it was a bug.

"Colt," Teegan said self-consciously, "we've been waiting for you to come home. We have decided to visit Rick and Ilsa at the shore. A friend told us that he was sick, and we feel we have to offer help. Ilsa and I grew up in the same family, and I need to be with her."

"Where's Ana?"

"She and Prof. Elvistine have gone to meet with his contact in the Conclave of Elders." As she spoke, Teegan shook her head *no*.

Colt swore, calling Ana several names, expanding his vituperation as Teegan nodded encouragingly.

Jordi held up a hand, stopping Colt. "Why don't you come with us to the shore?" he said. "Teegan can babysit Rick and Ilsa, and we can watch the ocean. Rick's house is big enough for all of us."

"Let me pack," Colt said. "It will teach her a lesson."

Colt packed a backpack with some clothes and toiletries. He put his cash tokens and access cards to Ana's credit accounts in a drawstring bag around his neck. Wondering if he was ever going to get some sleep, Colt, with Teegan and Jordi, left the apartment an hour later.

Once they were in the street, Colt looked for, but did not see, Linnet. The three friends hurried toward the subway nearest the apartment where, if they were going to the shore, the subway would take them through a city checkpoint and connect with the bullet train. Once enveloped in the noise of the subway, Jordi felt safe enough to speak without being overheard.

"Teegan and I are going to visit Rick and Ilsa just as we said. Arlo suggested strongly that we get out of town, and we are going to regardless of Teegan's reluctance." Teegan looked angry, but resigned. "Arlo showed up earlier with Ana, and she threw some clothes in a bag. He's the one who found the bug. He sprayed it with something to mess up the video, but couldn't do anything with the audio. They are going into the Subs. He told us to wait for you, then leave town."

"What did he find out?" Colt asked.

"We don't know, but he did stress that you should not wait to go downside. He said you were in danger." At that they parted. Teegan and Jordi caught the subway to the eastern checkpoint, and Colt disappeared into the Subs

15

Colt found Arlo and Piet seated at the table outside the trailer where they had met with Belasco the previous day. They were trying to comfort a distraught Ana, who was pacing and crying. When she saw Colt, she ran to him and threw her arms around him.

"I am so worried about the professor," she cried. "I know he is going to be hurt, maybe killed. He went to see Ara, his contact at the Conclave, by himself, without a guard or anything. They will try to stop him. They'll kill him."

Colt held her, sobbing, in his arms and murmured soothing noises. "Do you know what she's talking about?" Colt asked the two men. Arlo leaned on the table with his hands clasped in front of him. He looked as exhausted as Colt felt. "Ana is afraid Prof. Tillman and his boyfriend, Chandler Besdine, will try to keep Elvistine from reaching the Conclave. Tillman has been unsanctioned by the C.E. and sent to the stasis chambers. If Elvistine tells them he is at large, they will send their elite guard to kill him."

Piet looked interested. "What did this Tillman citizen do to be sent to the chambers?" he asked.

"Tillman was a colleague of Elvistine at the university. They had some kind of falling out, and Tillman embarked on a research project that he said proved that Elvistine's claim about opening a path between realities was a sham," Colt said.

"It's not, it's not," Ana almost stomped her foot. Colt continued to hold her and stroke her back in an effort to calm her.

Piet was clearly intrigued. "And that was enough for him to be unsanctioned? Usually the C.E. unsanction people for spreading false beliefs among the citizens; those beliefs being anything that contradicts the current teaching from the Conclave. Usually those beliefs don't include deep science which few citizens understand. Especially with respect to the portal, which is old news."

Arlo paced the floor, agitated. "All we know is the C.E. are committed to silencing Tillman." Arlo pounded his hands together. "I told him to lay low and keep out of sight. Someone in the C.E.'s inner circle is invested in keeping Elvistine's discovery unchallenged."

Piet shook his head. "It all seems far-fetched."

Ana pulled away from Colt and turned on Arlo. "You helped Tillman. I knew you were a traitor. How could you help that man? He's mad, a fanatic. His science is all wrong."

Arlo said sadly, "Prof. Tillman is one of my father's oldest friends. I don't know anything about his science, just that he is convinced the institute is being used for nefarious purposes."

"Nefarious purposes? What are you talking about?" Ana was scathing.

"He doesn't know, but he believes that Elvistine's contact in the Conclave was behind the reports that led to him being unsanctioned. If this situation were just a disagreement among scientists, no one would be in personal danger. The fact that the C.E. went so far as to send Tillman to the stasis chamber is convincing evidence that something important is going on. Despite the elders' insouciance about the rights of citizens, unsanctioning them for bad science is extreme."

"I take it this Tillman citizen did not enter the stasis chamber," Piet said.

Arlo just shrugged.

Colt said, "What about the demonstrators? They are threatening to destroy the institute, if not the university, because of deep science, because they think deep science will destroy the world. Tillman practices deep science. Maybe the C.E. are trying to pacify the demonstrators."

"Maybe. Their usual practice would be to send a unit of the army and annihilate them 'for the good of the citizens.'" Arlo continued pacing. "They could do that, but they have not.

"Besides, Elvistine practices deep science, too, and he is ostensibly the C.E.'s boy. It must have something to do with the damned portal."

Piet said, "If the C.E. are going to send in the army, they better act fast, the demonstrators are growing in number. They may be uninformed citizens who have been infected with mistaken beliefs, but someone is providing substantial amounts of funding to keep them going, to produce videos and provide cash and security for agitators to travel on recruitment missions. Then someone is providing passes for the recruits to come to the city. We are trying to identify the source of the and the motivation of the prime movers, unsuccessfully, so far."

"Why do you care?" Ana hissed at Piet Lem, who shrugged.

"When someone starts agitating the citizens, especially when someone agitates them to violence, I want to know who is doing it. The Subs would be vulnerable if a well- funded vigilante force threatened it. We have defenses, but many of our citizens are not able to protect themselves, and we might not be able to protect them. And I want to know what's going on in the city. Peace in the city ensures peace in the Subs."

"These materialists or anti-ephemerists or whatever they call themselves are threatening the institute, not the city," Colt said.

"For now, that's true. But groups like this, as they get bigger, become uncontrollable mobs that can be set off by any little thing. If they are successful in destroying the institute, they will be fueled with energy from their success and they will want to move on to other successes. They will not want to return to their dull lives in the countryside and the poorer sections of the cities. They could be manipulated or worse. They could just take fire from some random idea and go on a rampage. It could turn into a civil insurrection, then the C.E. would send in the military, and we would all suffer." Piet words worried Colt, who sensed that he knew more than he was saying.

"Fortunately, they are not armed," Colt said.

"Not yet, but arms earmarked for the group are beginning to flow through the Subs from other cities. I'm trying to divert them, but my attempts, so far, are not working. It isn't in the ethos of the Subs to interfere with citizens' trade. Not everyone downside shares my concerns. They don't care about the institute or the protesters. I think they lack foresight, but until enough of them become concerned, there is little I can do to stop the arms from flowing to the protesters."

Ana said, "I don't understand why the protesters don't fear the C.E. Are they so committed to their cause that they are willing to be martyrs?"

Arlo said, "She makes an interesting point."

"We have sources in the protest group," Piet said, and Colt and Arlo looked at each other as if to say *of course*.

"The protest leaders maintain that the C.E. supports their cause. The protesters believe that the C.E. will send assistance if they need it."

"Don't the protesters know the C.E. could just close the institute. They have the power to do anything they want to. They could unsanction it, and everyone and everything would vanish; the staff into re-education facilities and the equipment, the building itself, into a pile of rubble."

"They are told the C.E. welcomes their assistance, that the C.E. could do it if they chose, but they don't because they have them, the protesters, the enlightened ones, to take care of the issue. They are the C.E.'s special children, and the C.E. will reward them in the future."

"What reward?" Ana had stopped crying and appeared fascinated by Piet's account.

"The reward is not clearly stated. Just the idea that the C.E. is grateful is enough for many of the protesters. They are sure they will be rewarded."

"Where does the professor's contact live? Is his home in The Citadel with the C.E.? How is the professor traveling?" Colt changed the subject.

"He took the institute's aircar programmed with guidance from a travel satellite. Ara lives a few miles outside The Citadel." Ana began pacing again.

Colt turned to Arlo, "Would Tillman harm the professor? Or if he would, could he? Does he have his own followers?"

"Tillman would only harm Elvistine if he thought Elvistine seriously threatened him. If Elvistine goes to the C.E. and tells them Tillman is still alive and working on his research projects, Tillman would be in harm's way and he might try to stop him. Chandler Besdine would certainly do whatever is necessary to protect Tillman and not just because he is in danger himself. Chandler is convinced that Tillman's discoveries are crucial for the future of the planet."

"He's as bad as the anti-ephemerists if he believes some abstract discovery about the nature of space will harm the planet," Ana said contemptuously.

"He believes the planet is imminently in danger of being absorbed by a black hole and destroyed," Arlo said.

Ana was suddenly intrigued. "That's what Tillman's analysis indicates?"

"Yes. Does that have some bearing on the professor's findings?"

"There have been some recent anomalies in his measurements of the emanations from the portal."

"Emanations," Arlo laughed. "Is that a scientific

term?"

Ana made a face at him. "You may laugh, but determining the nature of the energy coming from the portal has eluded us so far. The professor thinks it might be a magnified neutrino effect, but so far we are unsure, so we just call them emanations. It's kind of an in-joke."

Colt brought them back to the moment. "My major focus is keeping Ana safe. Someone is trying to hurt her. We don't know who, and we don't know why. Personally, I only care because I want to neutralize any threat to her. I'm sure Arlo shares my concerns."

"And the professor," Ana said. "We must keep him safe."

"I don't care about the professor," Colt said. "He took off alone without protection, so he can take care of himself."

"You're right, Colt. I do care about Ana," Arlo paused for a moment—Colt thought he suddenly looked vulnerable—"and others, but I personally hope someone stops Elvistine from reaching ben Simeon and causing trouble for Prof. Tillman. He's just a scientist, like Elvistine, and he barely escaped with his life." Arlo looked unhappy.

"So you want someone to kill Desmond?" Ana was outraged.

Arlo grimaced. "Not killed, no. I don't want anyone to be killed. This whole situation is insane. I want us all to live in our little ivory towers and decode messages from other universes." He looked directly at Ana, "Or whatever it is that we do."

Ana started to say something, then paused. Both Arlo and Colt noticed her hesitation, but Piet had stood up and stretched.

"I don't know about you, but I need some sleep. We are all safe here for the time being. Let's have a meal, and then we will decide what needs to be done."

Ana looked like she was going to argue, but thought better of it. Colt was practically asleep on his feet, and Arlo was drawn and pale. Maybe getting some rest would provide clarity, or so they all hoped.

In the countryside outside the city, a bike equipped with a powerful fusion engine was zipping along carrying a lone rider whose posture expressed grim determination. Oren Mandible had slipped out of his home, Heartsease Asylum, early the previous morning headed for the city to find his wife and continue their life together. When she had fled the valley, he had believed he could remain happily among his family enjoying the peace and satisfaction of his home, safe from the chaos that lay without. But he had underestimated his love for Linnet and had discovered that life without her was unendurable. His oldest brother, sensing his pain, had given him the fusion bike and coordinates for the city and he was on his way to find her.

In her apartment, Irene was seething with frustration. Linnet was curled up on the couch, sucking her thumb, looking so utterly adorable that Irene could hardly restrain herself from curling up next to her and giving herself up to passion. Remy and Karin, her other roommates, *were* out doing the work of the organization, work that Irene should be doing rather than staying here thinking about sex.

Irene had had plans for Linnet, and her relationship with Colt Bede had been a pleasant surprise. But now Irene found herself in emotional turmoil because the entire situation had gone badly awry.

16

Piet generously allowed Colt and Ana to use the double bed in his trailer while he and Arlo bunked in with some of his Grupo compatriots. Colt was exhausted, but holding Ana in his arms was nice.

"It's been a long time since we were together like this," he said.

Ana sighed. "I know. I've been busy working. I miss you, and then the work just seems to take over."

He stroked her hair. "What was that comment Arlo made about the communication between universes? He said 'if that's what it is.' What did he mean? Doesn't Arlo believe in the portal?"

Ana sighed. "Arlo doesn't believe that I cracked the communication code."

"Did you?"

"Sort of." She shifted, played with her hair. He said nothing. "I can tell the pulses of energy coming through the portal are not random. They consist of patterns, subtly variable patterns like language. I just haven't been able to turn it into anything that corresponds with our language."

"What happens when you send messages through the portal?"

"The energy coming back intensifies; it feels angry. I thought it was better to tell people the message *was* threatening rather than that I interpreted it that way. Otherwise I am afraid they would try to intensify contact."

"Intensify how?"

"Try to send *things* through the portal. I have a feeling that could be dangerous. Then they might try to send things from their side."

Colt was intrigued. "Wouldn't that be interesting? Actual alien artifacts." He tried unsuccessfully to imagine what they might be.

"Look at it this way," Ana said. "We have already had one plague that wiped out a third of the population and brought about such disorder that we ended up with the entire planet and all its remaining peoples ruled by The Conclave of Elders. That was bad enough. Now you want objects from some parallel universe, or universes, bringing who-knows-what organisms through the portal."

"Maybe they just want to exchange information or would send wonderful things, cures for disease, free energy."

Ana leaned up on one elbow and looked intently at Colt. "Do you believe that?"

"No. I guess I don't."

She lay back down. "I don't either. The world has enough problems without adding to them from alternative universes. They might want information about us. I don't doubt that. But what if they are smarter than we are? What if they fear us and want to destroy us? What if they have their own protesters?"

She continued in a moody tone. "Elvistine lost interest in the portal. He moved on. Communication with space brothers is irrelevant in his world view. Once he has accomplished one goal, he develops another one. Now we are working on the proof that time cannot exist. The protesters would be crazy if they heard about that."

"How do you think Chandler heard about it," Colt asked, "if he has been in exile with Tillman?"

"We don't know that he has been in exile with Tillman. You met him here in the city. He may have been here all along, in contact with one of the boys or girls in the lab. They might have let something slip accidentally or on purpose. Who knows? They are not all completely devoted to Elvistine despite what he thinks."

"I suppose it's possible that Tillman sent him to the city to spy on the institute." Colt said.

"Why? Why would Tillman spy on Elvistine unless he thinks Elvistine framed him with the authorities? He might be thinking about revenge, sent Chandler to look for ammunition."

"Ana, do you think it possible that Elvistine did frame Tillman? You know him better than anyone."

"No. I don't think so. He was angry at Tillman, but he gets angry when people try to discount his work. He's a scientist, an academic, not a manipulator, except when it come to funding for the institute. Framing Tillman would not bring funding for the institute so I don't think he would do it."

Colt yawned. "I didn't tell you the whole of my conversation with Sparrow. Do you think Elvistine would contribute his sperm to a surrogate if he was offered enough funding for the institute?"

Ana laughed. A good sound that was missing from Colt's life lately.

"Now that's a question," she said.

Colt was asleep. Ana was still terribly worried about the professor, but exhaustion claimed her and she slept also.

The next morning they gathered around the familiar table in front of Piet's trailer. One of Piet's helpers, a thin, intense teenager, brought tea to the group, then joined the group. Piet Lem introduced him.

"This is my son Beau. We need to discuss what to do with you three. You can stay in the Subs indefinitely, but I'm not sure you want to. So far as I can tell, the authorities are not interested in any of you. They seem unaware that Arlo is back in the city. If you want to get out of the city without using a travel permit, Beau is your man." He smiled fondly at the young man, who gave him a cocky grin.

"We need to find out whether the professor reached ben Simeon safely. He would have arrived sometime during the past five hours, while we were sleeping. If he reached his contact, the C.E. will be aware that Tillman is alive, that he somehow escaped the stasis chamber. They will be looking for him."

"Once the authorities start looking for Tillman, I will know right away. Grupo tracks those of interest to the authorities. However, I can tell you one place he is not," Piet Lem said. "He is not in the Subs. My people have not been able to locate Chandler Besdine either. If Besdine is in the city, he is not staying under that name or contacting any known associates."

"It's a big city," Arlo said grimly.

"I met him playing Mah Jongg. I had never seen him before, but that's not unusual. It's a big network. Still if he was allowed to play, he must have contacts. They don't let people in off the street," Colt said.

"Beau and I can check that out. I don't personally have an interest in gaming but I can talk to a colleague who does. You said Chandler sported a fighting ball from his braid. That's rare enough to be remembered." Piet Lem continued. "Once we find him, we can invite him in for a chat.

"Ana, how will the professor get in touch with you? Your personal comm won't work down here."

"I left my personal comm in the apartment. You know the authorities can use them to track you. When he doesn't reach me on my comm, he'll contact the institute. We don't know that he is in danger from anyone except bandits in the countryside and the protesters, who seem to be located in the city. If he got through the countryside safely, he will be okay staying with his contact, right?" Ana had been speaking to Piet, but something in his face troubled her.

"You don't think he's safe," she said.

Piet shook his head. "I've been thinking about the protesters. They are well funded and organized and becoming more so every day. We know they are going to be armed soon, unless we in Grupo can find a way to stop that. What if they are being organized into an actual revolutionary party? They may have a secret policing group that we have not identified. It would be small at this point in their development, but it would make sense. Removing selected critics could be part of their plan. The professor is a highly visible target of the group. If he is killed, the power of the group is enhanced. The authorities might not be able to connect the group with his murder, but the popular opinion would readily connect the two."

"He could just disappear," Colt said.

"Not good enough. People who disappear can conceivably reappear. A disappearance lacks panache for the citizens. A good murder, however, is thrilling and controversial, especially if it is mysterious. You need to resurrect the ghost warriors." He smiled at Beau, who brightened at the mention of ghost warriors.

"Ghost warriors?" Ana was puzzled.

"In the old days, ghost warriors were secret assassins with paranormal skills who could go anywhere. No matter how secure the victim felt in his camp or castle, the ghost warriors would get in and kill him. They could climb walls like flies and were invisible."

Ana snorted. "Paranormal skills don't exist."

"Probably not," Piet Lem agreed, "but the ghost warriors were superbly conditioned and trained from childhood. Their abilities looked paranormal to the citizens, especially the citizen who thought he was completely safe until the ghost warrior dropped from the ceiling and beheaded him."

Beau laughed, and Ana looked alarmed. "You think the protesters have ghost warriors?"

"I'm just speculating. I think the protesters need increased attention from Grupo Uno. We have infiltrated at the lower levels, just to keep an eye on things, but I think we need to find out where the money is coming from."

"Piet, do you think the protesters are connected with the Command?" Arlo asked.

Piet Lem poured himself some tea. "I don't know if the Command exists. All we have is rumors. Someone says someone is disappearing citizens who patronize unsanctioned sex workers. Grupo has not heard of this. Someone else says citizens in the upper reaches of society who have unsanctioned habits are disappearing. Citizens in those circles do disappear, but usually money is the cause. Unsanctioned habits are, by their nature, not public knowledge and usually no one cares about another citizen's habits if the citizen is not threatening them. Arlo's young operative Cosmo says Remy admits being part of the Command, but his description of her does not comport with my idea of someone who disappears citizens. The name Command may be a bogey to misdirect attention, a sock puppet. You whisper that the Command are disappearing people, then X disappears, then you whisper that the Command disappeared X. If anyone cares, like the authorities, they are off searching for some mysterious group rather than at X's next of kin or business partners.

"Also, the protesters have no stated interest in perverts, to use an old term, or citizens catering to perverts. Probably if perverts and their agents are being disappeared, it is some other citizen vigilante group."

"Belasco said when the citizens in the higher social strata disappeared, the authorities did nothing," Colt reminded.

Piet Lem waved his hand dismissively. "Who can speak for the authorities? They don't answer to the citizens, so they can do what they want. Possibly they are carrying on their own investigation; possibly they disappeared the citizens themselves with orders from the C.E. We are merely speculating."

"We are no farther along than we were." Colt stood up, "Someone is asking questions about Ana and myself, someone is following Teegan and Jordi and possibly Ana. We have one lead, and that is Linnet. I'm going to find her and make her talk to me."

"Be careful," Arlo said. "Linnet is connected with Irene Thorne, and we know Irene Thorne disappears people, and she doesn't use mysterious groups to do it."

"As far as we know." Colt smiled at him.

"Take care of Ana," he said.

17

Colt did not go directly to the House of Blue Leaves
to search for Linnet. Instead he caught a subway
toward the sector of the city where the protesters had
their encampment, a site near the university where,
during the plague, an open space had been set aside
for disposal of the victims' bodies. A large facility had
been erected with assembly lines feeding the deceased
through the fusion chambers. All that remained of
each body was a few grams of dust. Once the plague
had been eradicated—no citizen knew exactly how
that happened, it had just disappeared—the chambers
had been dismantled and the space designated as a
park. It turned out the earth was contaminated with
chemicals and byproducts of the fusion process.
Landscaping had been unsuccessful and the city
authorities had abandoned the space to weeds and a
few feral cats and other small animals.

The protesters had turned the space into an
encampment with tents and makeshift huts.

Enterprising citizens had set up cafes and clubs and city authorities had established a clinic.

A sparse, prickly rain fell. In mid-morning, the sky was overcast, a dark opaque grey. Because of the superstition about rain spreading the plague, few residents were out and about, and none of them paid attention to Colt as he walked into the encampment. The alleys between the shacks were wide enough for a fusion bike or a small air car to navigate, but Colt saw none as he entered the outskirts of the camp. The buildings had a settled air; even the tents were built on platforms and looked substantial, comfortable. He could smell cooking from the cafes.

The network of streets quickly became confusing. The overall plan was a grid, and gradually he identified painted icons on paddles stuck in the corners for street signs. For citizens like Colt, who were literate in the old way, the icons were confusing until he noticed numbers indicating street coordinates incorporated within the patterns.

Feeling more comfortable now that he had an idea of how to track his location, he worked his way toward the center of the camp. Despite the rain, the number of citizens increased and the sound of voices intensified. In the distance, he thought he could hear a loudspeaker and gravitated in that direction, taking care to stay close to the walls of buildings and stepping out of the way of passersby. As he got closer to the center, he thought passersby were looking at him more carefully and noticed a couple who had badges and heavy batons that might indicate a policing function. He slowed his walk while trying to look purposeful, not an easy task, and found himself ducking into doorways. In one such doorway, as he paused to avoid two of the police-type citizens, he also avoided coming face to face with Chandler Besdine.

Colt was momentarily shocked at the sight, but recovered quickly as Chandler passed him, fighting ball still swinging gently from the pigtail down his back. Obviously comfortable within the camp, Chandler walked quickly, forcing Colt to step out of the doorway to catch sight of him turning a corner. Within the close confines of the camp, following unobtrusively was difficult, and Colt found himself wishing he was one of the ghost warriors they had discussed earlier. Smiling slightly to himself, he followed Chandler until he entered a large shack which had a sign outside indicating it was called the Banana Club.

Making a quick decision, Colt walked into the club as nonchalantly as possible. A bar ran down the left side of the room with small tables scattered along the other wall. The club was empty except for Chandler and a bartender who was a pretty, although no longer young, citizen; they seemed on very good terms.

As Colt approached the two, Chandler looked up with mock dismay.

"Oh, no, here's Colt Bede; come to get his money." He held out his fist for a fist-bump. "You must be here for the big match."

He turned back to the bartender. "Rusty, get my friend Colt a bourbon."

"I heard about the big match," Colt lied, "but I wasn't invited. I thought I would come down and look around." He raised his bourbon to Chandler and took a drink.

Chandler leaned forward confidentially. "I don't

know the details yet. I'm supposed to meet a contact at a certain location in a little while and get a pass. You can come with me; they will know you."

Colt was in a quandary. He could not become distracted by a big match even though he had more than the usual number of cash tokens in the sack around his neck. He now noticed their weight against his chest and grew a little warmer as adrenaline kicked in to his system.

"When I saw you down here, I thought maybe you were a supporter of the program." Colt waved a hand to indicate the camp.

Chandler frowned. "No, I'm just here for the MJ."

He looked around for the bartender, who had gone to the door and was looking out into the street. "Has Ana said anything to you about me?" he asked in a low voice.

"Only that you were in the advanced math department when she was. She said you were a protégé of Dr. Tillman."

"And Dr. Tillman is in a stasis chamber, having been declared unsanctioned and unsuitable for re-education." Chandler sounded bitter.

"Is he?"

"Why do you ask? Have you heard something about the professor?" Chandler was keeping his eyes on the bartender.

"Rumors, just rumors. Ana's colleague Elvistine is paranoid about Tillman. Some old academic disagreement. You might know more about that than I do."

"Oh, I know about it. I worked for Tillman. And it was more than a disagreement. The bastard Elvistine's supporters in the Conclave of Elders sent Tillman to the stasis chamber."

"You're saying Elvistine knew they were going to do that."

"He knew. Tillman's findings would prove that Elvistine's portal to an alternate universe was a sham."

"It's not a sham. Ana worked on the protocol that opened the portal and decoded the transmissions from the other side." He remembered what Ana had said about the portal, that she could not translate the messages. Was it possible she lied about the existence of the portal? Colt drank silently, thinking about the likelihood that Ana would lie to him. He loved her, and she loved him. She would not be the first person to lie to her beloved.

He and Ana had always had an unequal relationship in terms of their professional and intellectual achievements. He acknowledged Ana's brilliance. Everyone, including Ana, acknowledged Ana's brilliance. She might not regard lying to him about her research with Elvistine as a betrayal. Her loyalty to the institute was separate and apart from her loyalty to him.

Colt downed the rest of the bourbon.

Chandler brought him back to the moment. "Tillman didn't say that the portal didn't exist. He said it didn't communicate with an alternate universe."

"What did it communicate with if not an alternate universe? Pulses are constantly being received."

"Our calculations indicated that the portal must open up into a black hole." He grinned as Colt looked shocked. He had learned a little about black holes at the university. They were destroyers of universes. He actually remembered a video called *Black Holes: Destroyers of Universes.*

"On the other hand," Chandler said coyly, "Maybe only Elvistine can open a portal."

Colt did not follow up on this provocation, but was to remember it later.

Chandler continued. "The black hole Ana and Elvistine opened is tiny, at the ultra-subatomic string level. Now, if time does not exist, nothing would prevent the black hole from expanding to its fullest extent into our universe. Instantly."

Colt waved his hand again to encompass the surrounding camp. "So you are a believer with the protesters that deep science is dangerous."

Chandler sounded huffy. "If you are implying that I share the views of these idiots, you disrespect me. They conflate deep science and religion, and you know how everyone feels about religion. They think they can somehow stop the practice of deep science and that will remove the threat. Their leaders, whoever they are, are trying to shut down all theoretical inquiry. They seem to believe they can do that."

"And you don't think they can?"

"I think the C.E. supports deep science. Where do you think Elvistine's funds come from? He says wealthy donors. Name me donors wealthier than the Conclave of Elders. I know they funded Tillman's research."

Colt was having trouble processing this information. It presented so many questions that he could not answer. And he needed to find Linnet to ask her questions about Irene. He felt pulled in many directions, and at the back of his mind was the promise of the big game that Chandler had alluded to.

"Time to go meet my contact for the big game. You coming?" Chandler put a cash token on the bar and turned to go.

"No, I'm going to talk to Ana." Colt intended to, just not immediately. He disliked telling lies, and with Chandler, it seemed he did nothing else.

"You do that. It's a terrible thing to be lied to by your wife and her boss and probably everyone else." Chandler's smile was unpleasant.

"We need to talk again," Colt said. "Where can I find you?"

They had reached the door and Chandler hugged the bartender. "Rusty can always find me. Can't you, sweetheart?" She hugged him back and held out her fist to Colt for a fist-bump.

Out in the street, the rain continued to fall, but campers were hurrying toward the sound of the loudspeaker. Colt was of two minds, intrigued now by the protesters' program and curious what the campers were hurrying toward, but he decided to find Linnet first.

As Colt headed back toward the entertainment district and the House of Blue Leaves, the rain stuttered, then stopped entirely. The sky was still an opaque grey, but the streetlights had not switched on and all color was leached out of the landscape.

At the house, the gatekeeper waved him through, opening the wrought iron gate to the rickety elevator. The lounge was empty except for one of the boys, wearing only bikini briefs, sleeping on a couch. He jumped when the elevator opened and assumed a provocative pose until Colt, ignoring him, headed for the cafe.

Which was empty. Vague noises came from the kitchen, but nothing else stirred. The boy had almost gone back to sleep when Colt stood over him.

"My, you are handsome," the boy said.

"I'm looking for Sparrow."

"He's in the club. Take the elevator to the top floor." Colt walked toward the elevator, and the boy called, "It's slow today. I could give you half price."

The end of a perfect day, Colt thought, half-price sex.

The club encompassed almost the entire top floor of the building, but its extent was difficult to estimate because it was painted dark blue with leaves outlined in silver and dotted with small silver lights. A bar encircled two walls on one level; then stairs led up to a second level, which held tables and private booths. Like most clubs of this type, platforms could be raised from floor level holding dancers and performers, leaving the ground floor open for dancing.

Usually the room would be vibrating to music, but this afternoon it was quiet. A bartender sat in a corner of one of the bars watching army/navy cage fighting on a video box. Upstairs lights shone in two of the private booths, but the customers were invisible. On the main level, one table was occupied by several citizens. Sparrow, rising, recognized Colt by his ubiquitous backpack, then the blond hair. He raised an arm and called out, catching Colt's eye.

The table held an assortment of small plates, one of which seemed to hold real organic scallops. Several bottles were dotted around the table at which four people were seated: Sparrow and three citizens who looked to Colt like prosperous businessmen. At first Colt thought they might be customers, but Sparrow introduced them by name.

"Please excuse the interruption," he said to them when the introductions were finished. "Colt and I are mutually concerned about one of my girls. She seems to have become entangled with bad company, and since she is a country mouse, unfamiliar with our city ways, we want to keep her safe."

"Keeping good employees is difficult," pronounced a pompous citizen, introduced as Desmond, who looked like he spent a lot of time at spas.

Sparrow laughed. "This particular employee was one of the worst I have ever trained. She had no aptitude at all for pleasure with citizens of either gender. She was competent; all my workers are competent. I train them myself, but she couldn't muster up a bit of enthusiasm."

"You tried aphrodisiacs?" Desmond said, as if to imply, *as would anyone.*

"Yes, but they are too intense," Sparrow said. "I try to use them only on request or for some of our older customers. They didn't do much for our country mouse. She had no trouble consummating the act. She just didn't like it."

"Sounds like my wife," someone said, and they all laughed.

A man, introduced as Xander, wearing an elegant woven black silk necklace with a silver fitting, said "I have some new herb-based gels that are excellent external stimulants, much more natural than drugs. I'll send you over a sample." He mentioned the name of a supplier.

Sparrow nodded graciously.

"Your girl sounds perfect for the surrogate trade if she's healthy. Coming from the country, she might be able to carry a child to term. Her fortune and yours, as her agent, would be made," suggested a small man with hair too beautiful to be natural.

"I was considering what you say, St. John, when she started going AWOL. Her friends in the house thought she had fallen in love, but I found that difficult to believe. We all fall in love from time to time," they all nodded vigorously, "but there needs to be a strong attraction. This Linnet seemed incapable of a strong attraction, especially to a barracuda like Irene Thorne."

The man named St. John put a hand on Sparrow's arm. "Irene Thorne," he cried. "If she's mixed up with that woman, let her go." All the men around the table nodded, except Xander, who said, reminiscently, "I knew her father." This comment brought respectful looks from the other men.

"My father and he were at school together. He was a fine man, brilliant, entrepreneurial, a died-in-the-wool materialist. Always surrounded by the most beautiful women, the finest food, wine, art. The best of everything. His businesses are still among the strongest in the world. Irene would have inherited them, but she and her father had a fight just before he died, and they went to her brothers."

"Possibly the C.E. would not let her inherit anyway," the man called St. John said. "There were rumors that she was being investigated."

"For what?" Sparrow said. "I had not heard that."

"No one knew for sure. She had taken over her

law firm in a few short years and cemented its relationship with the city authorities and the C.E. At least that is what people thought. A few people had disappeared who might have stood in her way, but the authorities blamed citizens of the Subs and did nothing. It was enough to make people nervous around her. Then there were subtle rumors that she was being watched, evaluated. Then in a very short period of time, she had a big fight with her father, he died, and she left the firm."

"What is she doing now, besides seducing Sparrow's country mouse?" St. John asked.

"No one knows. She dropped out of society. So for people in those circles she might as well be dead," Xander said.

"Well, she inherited a boatload of money from her mother, so she is not waiting tables somewhere," Sparrow said. "Enough money to disappear any number of people, including myself and you, friend Colt. I am thinking you should let Linnet go. You don't want to find yourself vaporized by one of Irene's hirelings from the Subs."

Colt shook his head. "There is some indication that Irene has targeted my wife and myself. We have no idea why except that my wife is a fellow at the Institute for Temporal Epistemology, and the anti-ephemerist protesters have targeted the institute." He addressed the three men at the table. "Do any of you know if Irene has anti-e proclivities?"

St. John looked interested. "Her father was an avid materialist, completely anti-e, and I always thought Irene was also. It's almost *de rigueur* in some circles, but if she had gone over to the ephemerist camp, that would explain her father's anger."

"That would not explain why she would target your wife and the institute. Are you sure it is her?" Xander asked, interested in spite of himself.

"So it seems. We are being followed by citizens with a connection to her." Colt thought it wiser not to mention Linnet in this role. "We think perhaps she selected Linnet for attention because she knew Linnet was connected with me."

"Actually," Sparrow said, "your relationship with Linnet may be just a happy accident. I think I can explain how she became aware of Linnet. It was recently noticed that one of my employees was spending more money than he should based on his salary. Which, I might add, is quite adequate for what he does." He looked around to see if anyone would question his treatment of his employees. No one did.

"When we questioned him, he admitted that Irene Thorne had a standing offer of money, old money, for tips on fertile young girls from the country. She specified the age and where the girl must come from. He had informed her about Linnet as soon as her fertility tests were confirmed."

"Some people believe girls from certain areas are more fertile," one of the men observed. "I myself am skeptical."

Xander turned to Colt. "Well, you can rest easy on one count at least. If you are being followed and you know it, you are not under investigation by the authorities. They never reveal themselves during their investigations until the middle of the night, the knock on the door."

Colt gave Xander a dark look. "The authorities have nothing to investigate us for."

"That's never stopped them," Xander observed,

unmoved by Colt's anger.

"Enough," Sparrow said. "We must get back to business. Clientele will be pouring in soon, and my compatriots need to get back to their own businesses. Colt, I have heard nothing from Linnet. If I do, I will contact you immediately. I will even, if humanly possible, try to keep her here, but I can't tangle with Irene Thorne."

"Thanks," Colt said, spearing the scallop he had been eyeing; it was soy analogue, delicious but not organic. "I'll be taking off." He hoisted his backpack and left the gentlemen to their business.

On his way back to the Subs, he stopped at a public kiosk and called an answering service used by Piet Lem for upside business. Yes, he was told, there were messages for him if he would give the password. He did and received a simple one-sentence message.

Dr. Elvistine has dropped out of sight.

\

18

Colt hurried back to Grupo headquarters to find Ana in hysterics and poor Beau trying to comfort her. Piet Lem and Arlo were elsewhere; Beau said he didn't know where. Ana had received the word about Elvistine via one of Piet's secure communication links. The caller knew only that a representative of ben Simeon, Elvistine's contact at the Conclave, had sent a message to the institute that the professor had not reached ben Simeon's village. He was concerned because an agitated Elvistine had not divulged why he was rushing to see him.

BenSimeon's representative was going to notify the authorities that patrolled the countryside to keep an eye out for the air car. A crashed air car would be cannibalized almost immediately if found, but certain areas were sparsely populated so wreckage might lay unmolested for some time.

Tired of ineffectually patting Ana on the shoulder while she alternated screaming and crying, Beau released her to Colt, who did no better. Finally Beau brought over a healer from the Subs, a toothless elderly citizen who slapped a narcotic patch on her neck that knocked her out.

"She's really upset," Beau understated. "Is he her father or something?"

"They have worked together for a long time."

"All that crying seems a little extreme to me. Are women like that all the time?"

Colt, too, thought the crying was a little extreme, especially for someone as phlegmatic as Ana, but he was not going to discuss his opinion with this kid. All he could offer was the dubious reassurance that most women are pretty weird.

The kid nodded his head wisely. "Father M said you are better off without a partner. He said celibacy is the way for Osirans; it improves your ability to meditate."

"What's an Osiran and who's Father M?"

The kid looked surprised, realizing he was guilty of violating a basic rule of the Subs, talking too much to strangers. He started to say something, but Colt put up a hand and said, "Don't tell me. I don't care about anything except keeping Ana safe."

Relieved, Beau said, "Arlo got word that one of his friends—I guess he was a friend even if he was a digger—had been killed. His name was Cosmo something. He had done some work for Arlo."

"Did Arlo say what kind of work?"

"No. He just swore a lot and left in a hurry."

Colt moved his backpack off a chair and sat down at the table which held a couple small plates with crackers and fruit, hummus, and a bottle of wine. Normally he didn't drink wine, but given the craziness of the past few days, he poured himself a glass. Beau sat down across from him and ate an olive.

"I guess you didn't see Linnet?" he said.

"No. She is among the many missing, but at least she seems to be alive." The wine tasted like a pine tree, a really old pine tree, but he could sense the kick. He ate a cracker and some hummus. Trying to sound casual, he said, "What exactly is Arlo doing back in the city? I thought he was avoiding the authorities, that he had been declared unsanctioned."

The kid looked surprised. "Didn't he tell you?"

"I've hardly had time to see him since he got back. He blew into town, told some people he wanted to see us; then all this craziness started happening." He had another glass of wine; it was tasting slightly better. He could get to like it.

"I don't know either. My dad just said he was a friend of the Grupo and to do whatever he said. Since he had never said that before, I assumed that Arlo was doing something important. So far he has not asked me to do anything but be ready to take one or more people out of the city without leaving a trail."

Colt leaned confidentially toward the kid, trying to project solid vitality and trustworthiness.

"Beau, do you know anyone downside that could construct an explosive device for me?" he whispered.

Drawn, Beau leaned forward himself, forgetting that he was surrounded by solid rock and protected by all his father's formidable defenses, "You mean a bomb?" he breathed.

"Yes. A small one, but one that could do a lot of damage."

"Like a fusion device."

"Like that." Colt had no idea what a fusion device

consisted of.

"You want one?" the kid asked, impressed.

"I might. How much would one or two of them cost?"

The kid leaned back, trying to look like a player. "I could find out."

"You do that," Colt said. "And, kid, this is just between you and me, right?"

The kid was on his feet, already tasting the middleman fee, "Sure," he said, "sure."

Colt tossed the rest of his glass of wine in a slop pail and shouldered his backpack. It was tasting good, but he needed to stay sober, needed to move. He couldn't stand sitting around the empty cavern by himself. He checked on Ana, who was asleep and, according to the healer, would be out for another eight to ten hours. They had left the patch on her neck to help keep her under.

Moving confidently through the tunnels, Colt headed for a distant entrance, one that would drop him near the protesters' camp. His plan was to see Chandler, try to determine whether he knew anything about Elvistine's whereabouts. Chandler and Arlo were both close to Tillman; Chandler might know what Arlo was up to.

In college Arlo had been the student with the interesting ideas, the interesting friends; a natural networker, he mingled with students from other cities, hung out with professors, and he would brag about his familiarity with the Subs. Most citizens thought the Subs were a myth but those were not the people Arlo cultivated. Not athletic, he had friends in ROTC; not artistic, he had friends in the art and museum departments. He had become their suite-mate through the mysterious assignment process universities use and opened their eyes to a larger world than they could have imagined.

His admission to the Marketing and Propaganda Program—MarkiProp the students called it—provided automatic assurance that he was well-connected and his family and school years blemish free. Colt found out later most of the records were false, but at the time, he did not know such things were possible and he had been impressed. Equally impressive was Arlo's reputation for possessing extraordinary talents, mysterious capabilities. The exact nature of his attributes was vague, varying from group to group, and always described at secondhand. That he was special was clear to everyone, especially Arlo.

Being in the Marketing and Propaganda Program afforded Arlo training in the manipulation of facts and images. Colt often thought Arlo embodied his field of study as few students did.

Ten years ago the New Dispensation was maturing although the C.E. were still consolidating their hold on the planet. Control had been easy to establish in those countries hit hardest by the plague. But in locations where fewer people had died, resistance to the new regime was vigorous, though ultimately doomed.

The Conclave of Elders had taken credit for stopping the plague. No one knew how that had been accomplished, just as no one really knew what caused it.

From the beginning, speculating that the C.E. might be responsible for starting the plague themselves was a quick ticket to the nastier re-education facilities if not a stasis chamber.

The plague was finished; that was enough for most citizens. Then the C.E. had abolished religion on the grounds that God would have stopped the plague had He existed. They answered the religionists, who had argued that the plague was sent by God to warn people that they had descended into sin and strayed from the true path, etc. The C.E. simply said that any god worth worshipping would never do something like that, that even though a god had not instigated the plague, it was naturally occurring; an omnipotent god could have stopped it, but did not. Therefore God did not exist. Therefore religion was a sham. Therefore the practice of religion was forbidden, and the preaching of religion was dissemination of unsanctioned thought and a one-way ticket to re-education facilities. Citizens quickly observed that these were re-education facilities from which few people returned.

Possibly the fact that the religionists were the most organized and effective groups fighting the C.E. had contributed to their decision. Speculating on that topic was not healthy and seldom indulged in outside the universities. The C.E. cut the students some slack—they needed educated people badly—but they were less indulgent of common citizens who still had some residual fondness for their old belief systems.

Fanatics, citizens loudly preaching for their particular belief system, who began demonstrating in the cities, who in one case led a crusade against the Conclave of Elders, disappeared into the re-education facilities in droves. Occasionally one would acquire a significant reputation or accomplish a particularly flamboyant act, the leaders of the crusade on the Conclave for example, and would be sent to the stasis chamber. Under the New Dispensation no one was executed. That was a throwback to a backward barbaric time. Under the New Dispensation one guilty of sufficiently unsanctioned thoughts or extreme unsanctioned actions or both went into a stasis chamber where one would be held in suspended animation, theoretically forever, or until the C.E. approved reanimation. So far no one had been reanimated.

The somewhat simplistic philosophy of the C.E. was much discussed by students in the universities. They poked holes in the C.E.'s arguments and disdained their logic.

Other students were more interested in the history of the C.E. Prior to the plague, they were a well-known secular fraternal organization, international in scope, that provided extensive educational and medical assistance in the form of schools, hospitals, and clinics worldwide. Then the plague began and people died in the streets. The onset seemed vaguely connected with unusual weather systems. Rain fell in desert areas and on high plateaus where some inhabitants had never seen it. Animals as well as humans fell victim to the plague.

Governments were unable to cope with the resulting chaos, but the C.E. had stepped in. It was miraculous, really, how efficiently they established institutions and infrastructure to help citizens adjust. The C.E. was not local. Individual countries were simply abolished. Citizens were now citizens of the planet, which was better for everyone; the C.E. knew citizens would agree. One language was established for education and commerce, and the C.E. had their own military, originally established, they said, to protect the organizations myriad institutions from hostile local inhabitants. The military was well-funded and armed and the indigenous military groups were quickly co-opted. In return for supporting the C.E., local military groups were rewarded, receiving control of farms, industries, and corporations where the owners had succumbed to the plague.

Arlo was a participant in intense study and discussions of the rise, the apotheosis of the C.E. Groups of MarkiProp students would gather in all-nighters, talking about how it was that the C.E. had gone from a benign multinational NGO to the ruler of the planet. The identity of the C.E., their number, even the location of The Conclave, as the ruling body was called, were unclear. School children were taught from little books with pictures of golden skinned men and women, bald but with artistic tattoos in their third eye region, wearing long white robes. The C.E., they were taught, had stepped up when the plague erupted and taken control of the planet *for the good of the citizens* and when order was restored to the planet . . . something would happen.

One side effect of the plague was decreased fertility among women. Fewer women could carry a fetus to term, and a diminished birth rate exacerbated the problems flowing from the reduced population. Most children were now conceived using surrogates residing in baby farms in the countryside, which was thought to have a more salubrious climate.

Schools were available in the cities, especially for wealthy families, but children who were adopted from the baby farms often remained there and were raised entirely at the expense of the C.E. Many parents satisfied with weekend jaunts to the countryside to see their children. Multiple-child families were rare because the availability of surrogates was limited. Surrogates could literally name their price.

Arlo and his friends had grown to hate this system. They felt that the human need for self determination had been quashed. They regretted the loss of religion, Arlo especially, when he secretly converted to the Osiran belief system.

The students closest to Arlo became more militant, at least conceptually, until a defining moment when one of the members, Isabel Caliente, was uncovered as a police spy. Isabel was very close to turning in members of the group to the authorities, accusing them of unsanctioned beliefs. No one suspected her, and she would have succeeded had she not fallen in love with one of the members, Max Sforza, and warned him that he was in danger of being revealed. Max immediately sold her out to the group.

Frightened and angry, Arlo arranged for the core of the group to meet with Piet Lem in the Subs where they could flee if they needed to. At that meeting, Piet had proposed to the stunned students that the simple solution to the problem was for the lover to continue to romance the spy, determining how much information she had already imparted to her superiors. Depending on how much she had spilled, they could take the simplest route; she could be disappeared.

Although the group agonized over the cold-blooded nature of this approach, ultimately they saw it as viable. Isabel told Max that she had not been assigned to a specific group on campus, rather she was part of the apparatus the authorities used to monitor students. And she had not delivered her report on Arlo and his friends. Thus, one day Isabel was walking through a park near campus, watching a group of students play croquet, and then she was gone. Her superiors in the city authority were suspicious. But with no information to act on, they could only recruit another spy.

Arlo had told Colt about the disappearance; they both knew Isabel from class. Colt had been shocked, then outraged, at the murder. Colt saw immediately that if Arlo got into trouble, he would drag Ana with him. Her interests always focused on her work more than any of the roommates except Arlo. The two were especially close and everyone, except possibly Ana, knew that Arlo was in love with her. Colt himself had been in love with Ana since their first year as suite-mates.

Then Arlo and his friends started throwing bombs.

19

Colt found out about the bomb throwing by accident one night when he was in the Subs playing Mah Jongg. It was early in his gambling career, the bug had not infiltrated his system quite so deeply, and he could still think about not spending all his time and money in over-lit rooms with people who stank.

He was heading to a tournament very late and worrying a little bit about a martial arts class he would probably miss the next day. He was due to be tested for another belt, one he needed if he was to get into the military. This career path was becoming less appealing than it had once been. He had been a champion athlete in secondary school and excelled in college, so he should have been a shoo-in. Amass a couple more belts and he would have a permanent, comfortable gig on an army or navy sports team. He might even compete in martial arts or cage-fighting. He was good, but he had lost interest. He could never figure out whether the fighting was too easy or too hard.

Grumbling to himself, he stopped to take a whiff of kampour, an illegal drug he had recently started using and which provided a brief respite from worrying about whether Ana would ever love him and what he would do with his life after college. Oh, yes, and how he could recoup some of his recent gambling losses.

In this mood he almost passed the door of one of the little noodle shops that appeared from time to time in the Subs. The smell that emanated from these shops was fantastic, almost mystical, and Colt was not immune. He stopped and stepped backward, noticing a split second before he entered that his roommate Arlo was already there, chatting with the proprietor as he stirred a huge pot of soup. Colt might have barreled into the place and had a bowl of noodles with Arlo except for the citizen Arlo was so intently listening to. He was an older man, easily in his 50s, so he had survived the plague as an adult. Younger citizens were a little wary of such people. It was almost as if they were from a different dimension. Colt had thought it typical of Arlo to befriend such a person. Plus the citizen had a beard, not an unsanctioned adornment exactly, but discouraged by the authorities, and not just an ordinary beard. This beard grew down to the vicinity of the citizen's breastbone in a greyish, curly mass and had been split so that it swept in two equal wings. This type of personal excess was not in keeping with the C.E.'s mandates about simplicity of dress and personal appearance. Bright colors and jewelry were discouraged, the latter excepted for the wealthy classes, and artificial hair color and unusual beards were discouraged and could bring unwanted attention.

Since the citizen Arlo was chatting with would draw all kinds of unwanted attention upside, Colt concluded he was one of the residents of the Subs who never left. He was unusual, and Colt was a child of his times. Anything unusual was curious, interesting, ultimately suspect, and to be avoided. He had avoided the noodle shop that evening and gone on to the match.

When Colt next saw the man with the split beard, he was dead, a victim of the officers who had caught him just after he left a bomb that exploded inside the police station. Numerous people had been killed. The citizen had been brought in for a chat about his unsanctioned personal adornment and smuggled the tiny fusion bomb into the station—in the beard. Through a series of unfortunate accidents, he had been caught and summarily shot. His picture was in all the video reports with denunciations and orders for anyone knowing him to report to the police. Colt was scared to death.

Arlo had reassured him. The bomb thrower, a citizen named Eustis Hollowell, had been killed before he could tell the authorities anything. The authorities were assuming he had acted alone because of a personal grudge he had against the police.

Arlo confided to Colt that Eustis had, in fact, had a personal grudge against that particular police station and had chosen the target himself. In the near future, Arlo had said, other sites in this and other cities would be blown up and manifestoes would be circulated about how the C.E. was not protecting citizens and asking difficult questions about the C.E.

and its plans for the planet. Arlo and his friends assumed citizens would then become aware to their lack of freedom, rise up against the iron fist of the C.E., etc.

When Colt expressed his concerns about Ana and the other suitemates, Arlo assured him they would be safe. The group Arlo had joined had powerful friends in the upper reaches of society, friends who were disenchanted with the rule of the C.E., with the taxation and constant surveillance.

Colt had been unconvinced, but matters had come to a head quickly. A failed bombing of an elementary school had led to the arrest and interrogation of one of the group. The combination of sleep deprivation and powerful psychoactive drugs had revealed the names of the most active members of the group, including Arlo, and he and Max Sforza had fled into the countryside.

Although under the deepest suspicion, the suitemates were able to convince the authorities that they knew nothing about Arlo's activities.

Colt, the only one who did know anything, received only summary questioning because he was then involved in the military Olympics, successfully defeating numerous opponents to finally emerge as the third greatest cage-fighter in the world. The win had ensured his place in the army when he graduated and protected him from suspicion. A segment of the citizenry had begun to adulate athletic heroes and project upon them purity of purpose and loyalty to the C.E. and the New Dispensation. Colt appreciated the irony that this trend had been a major effort of Arlo's department, MarkiProp.

As Colt had hoped, Ana had turned to him for

comfort after Arlo was declared unsanctioned. They had been married right after graduation, Teegan and Jordi as their attendants. Dr. Elvistine, who was now Ana's mentor as well as employer, gave the bride away.

Now Arlo was back, acting as if nothing had happened, talking about an unspecified threat to Ana and Colt. Despite the talk, all that had happened to Colt and Ana so far was people asking questions of the building attendant and Linnet following Teegan and Jordi.

Colt was beginning to wonder if the threat was serious. He felt like he was being set up, and he was troubled by Beau's assurance that he could supply fusion bombs. Beau had seemed too casual about the question, too ready to deal.

In the protesters' encampment, finding the makeshift club where he had met Chandler was easier than Colt expected. Rusty, the bartender, recognized him and acknowledged him, unsmiling, nodding toward the back of the room toward a curtained doorway. Colt went through the doorway and on through the kitchen to a second door, this time of wood, that opened to reveal a small apartment with a table and futon. Chandler sat at the table.

Behind him, Colt sensed a presence. His martial arts training kicked in and he dropped to the ground, attacking from below. A grunt of pain erupted as he twisted a leg. The assailant's body fell on him, and before he could inflict significant damage, he felt a cold object pressed against his head.

"Do you know what this is?" a voice asked.

"A fusion pistol," Colt said. He twisted the foot he

held, causing its owner to yelp.

"Let him go or I will push the button," the voice said.

"We don't want to hurt you," Chandler said from across the room.

"Shut up," the voice said.

Colt released the foot, giving it a little tweak to stretch the tendons. The coldness receded from his head and the voice said, "I also have a conventional weapon that will kill you just as dead as the fusion pistol. Stand up and go sit on the bed."

Colt jumped to his feet, considering an attack. He was fully capable of taking out three or four people, even if they were armed, especially if they were as inept as the guy who was rocking in pain on the floor. He was unclear about Chandler's ability. He did sport the fighting ball, but that didn't mean he knew what to do with it. He was more concerned about the other party in the room.

Although he had never been given a description, he knew her immediately. "Irene Thorne," he said.

She was holding a conventional composite pistol with every appearance of ease. The fusion pistol had disappeared, probably in the handbag next to her. "Colt Bede. We meet at last. Pelham here has been giving me reports about your activities." She nodded toward the sound of moaning.

"Teegan and Jordi told me about you," Colt said to Pelham. "You brought a message from Arlo."

"Pelham's a consummate gofer," Irene said.

"Cosmo Naftali was a gofer, too, and he's dead," Colt said.

Pelham looked at Irene, then Chandler, for confirmation. "Nothing to do with us," Irene said.

"Just a coincidence." Her tone was not convincing.

Pelham forced himself to his feet. "Still, if you are through with me, I'll be going."

Irene turned the gun toward him, and Colt easily snatched it from her hand, unloaded it, and put the bullets in his pocket.

Irene started to cry and tried to reach inside the large handbag.

Colt tossed the pistol at her arm, knocking it away from the bag. "Let's all keep our hands in plain sight and not make any sudden moves. I really can kill all three of you with my bare hands in about 90 seconds."

Irene snuffled. "What are you? Some kind of ghost warrior?"

"He was once a champion army Olympian," Chandler said. Colt didn't care for the way he emphasized the word *once*.

He said, "Pelham, give Irene something to blow her nose with."

Pelham looked around ineffectually, then pulled back the curtain and handed her a dirty dishtowel.

For some reason, this made her cry harder.

"Can I go now?" Pelham whined.

"No," Colt said. "Sit down and shut up. You've been following me. Why?"

"She paid me, but she didn't say why."

"Did you follow me in the Subs?" And if you did, Colt asked himself, why didn't my friends in the Subs see you?

"No. She said that wasn't necessary."

"Why wasn't it necessary, Irene? Do you have other contacts in the Subs?"

"I don't have to answer your questions." She blew

her nose defiantly in the dirty dishcloth. Before she could do anything else, Colt had her by the hair with a knife at her throat.

"You *do* have to answer my questions."

"I have contacts who know Beau Lem. He talks about you."

"Now for the more important question. Why are you interested in me and, more importantly, Ana?" He twisted her hair a little tighter so that her head was pulled back at an uncomfortable angle.

"I need you. I'll pay you anything you want. You can help me destroy Desmond Elvistine."

Colt was taken aback. "The professor? Why? Because he's an ephemerist?"

"I have personal reasons." Colt admired how she could sound so offended with a knife at her throat. "I'll tell you what you want to know; just let go of my hair."

Colt pushed her into a chair and stepped back so he was leaning against the wall. Irene shook her head a couple time and sat on the bed, rubbing her neck.

"I did not intend to cause any problems for you. I wanted to talk with you, make you both an offer, a very good offer. I still want to. I know what you both want, and I could provide it. You want unlimited funds to gamble, and Ana wants to continue the work of the institute. You could have both."

"Not if the work Elvistine has accomplished is invalidated. If Elvistine is disgraced, the institute will lost all its prestige."

"You don't understand," Irene said militantly. "I'm not interested in his work at the institute. Ana can continue the ridiculous project about the abolishment of time that she is working on." Colt noticed

Chandler make a protesting gesture when she made this statement. "I am interested in the portal. We must convince the C.E. that the portal is a sham, that it does not exist, that Elvistine created the story about it to show up Tillman." She looked at him beseechingly. "The portal is dangerous."

"You mean because it is a black hole and enlarging it could destroy the world? Chandler told me about that."

"There are factions among the elders in the C.E. Most of them realize that the portal is potentially dangerous and want to take a cautious approach. They are not completely convinced of the danger, but they are willing to leave it alone and proceed according to a careful protocol.

"Another faction, an increasingly powerful faction, not only wants to enlarge it, they want to send someone through it. They want to find out what's involved in exploring it. They have dominated this planet; now they want to dominate the universe.

"But we know if they expand the existing portal or open another one, this planet will be destroyed." To Colt she sounded convinced of the truth of this far-fetched assertion.

Irene continued. "If we can convince the C.E. that Elvistine is a nut, that he imagined the whole thing, they will all turn their attention elsewhere. They have universities working on interplanetary travel."

"You could simply disappear Elvistine."

"No, no," she said, looking away. "We need to keep Elvistine alive."

"Your contacts may have let you down for once," Colt said. "You don't know that Elvistine has dropped out of sight. He was on his way to see his contact at the C.E., and he disappeared, hopefully not permanently."

Irene jumped up, suddenly agitated. "How was he traveling?"

Colt told her about the air car. "Well, that is a dangerous way to travel without bodyguards. He could have been stopped by bandits or a local militia."

"But this could be terrible," she said. "Why was he on his way to C.E. headquarters?"

"He came to suspect that Tillman was at large, and he wanted to warn the C.E. He felt he had to do it in person, to stress the importance of tracking Tillman down and neutralizing him. He has a lot of faith in his importance to the C.E."

Irene ran her fingers through her hair and muttered *this is terrible* three or four more times. "Don't you see what happened? Word that Elvistine was coming reached the C.E., at least those in the C.E. who want to use the portal, and they decided to fake his disappearance while he opened another portal for them. They have all the necessary equipment in one of their laboratories."

"Elvistine can't open a portal without Ana," Chandler said, lying confidently.

"Ana didn't go with him?" Irene said anxiously.

"No." Colt said, "Ana's safe in the Subs with Piet Lem."

Chandler looked doubtfully at Colt. "Are you sure? If the C.E. put a big enough bounty on her, there are people in the Subs who would go against Piet Lem to kidnap her. Efficient, remorseless people. Irene knows them better than I do."

Colt looked at Irene. "Is that true?"

"I have used the services of one group in the past,

but I don't know if they would kidnap Ana. They won't usually target women?"

"Are they some kind of religionists?" Colt asked.

"No, they are all women. They have a thing about disappearing women."

"I have heard a lot about your past, Irene. Surely you have been responsible for disappearing women," Colt said.

"Yes, but very few. I generally use Pelham for that."

Pelham, who was leaning his chair against the wall on its back two legs, dropped forward and looked discomfited at her comment.

Irene said, "But I don't know every bad citizen in the Subs. We need to make sure Ana is safe. Colt, you and Chandler return to Piet Lem and make sure he knows how important it is to protect Ana. Pelham and I have work to do here."

Colt briefly wondered what work Irene had to do in the protesters' camp, but he was focused on getting back to Ana.

He picked up his backpack, taking the fusion pistol from Irene's handbag but leaving the conventional gun behind. Pelham tried to protest when he took the fusion pistol, which was intrinsically valuable and essential for Pelham's occupation, but Colt ignored him. A fusion pistol could come in very handy.

"You come with me," he said to Chandler. "I want to keep an eye on you."

Completely relaxed, Chandler picked up his shoulder bag and preceded Colt through the door.

When Colt and Chandler returned to Piet Lem's trailer, they found him listening carefully to a report from one of the members of Grupo, a young man of his son Beau's generation. Colt ignored them and hurried into the trailer, which was empty and Ana's things were missing. Outside again, he went to Piet Lem and, interrupting the reports, demanded to know where Ana had gone.

Piet Lem said she got a message from Elvistine stating that he desperately needed her help. Elvistine had been ambushed by bandits and had managed to escape in the confusion when another group came to challenge the first group for the air car. He had made it to a village called Niebuhr and called Ana. She had left immediately after she received the message, telling Piet Lem she would not wait for Colt, that she would hire a livery service. Livery services provide pricy but safe transportation in the countryside when train service is not convenient. Piet Lem had insisted Beau go with her since she and Beau both had authorized passes out of the city.

She had promised Piet Lem she would contact him immediately when she had picked up Elvistine and headed back to town.

Feeling somewhat relieved, Colt threw his backpack on the ground, and Chandler threw his messenger bag next to it.

The Grupo member had been waiting patiently for Piet Lem to finish his conversation, started to say something, but Piet Lem silenced him. "First, let's let Colt introduce his friend."

Colt introduced Chandler Besdine to Piet Lem, who said, "And this is Hicks, one of my best men." Hicks, who looked to be about fourteen, grew an inch before their eyes, inclined his head to Piet Lem.

"Hicks has been keeping an eye on the protesters

for us." Piet Lem said. "He reports that they expect the delivery of arms in a very short timeframe, but no one seems quite clear on what they are going to do with them. He also reports that they are adding new recruits to the program daily and he believes, based on their accent, that they are not from the city."

"Where does he think they are from, and do they appear to have military training?" Chandler chimed in.

"Somewhere in the far south of here is his best guess. He has been reluctant to ask too many questions. He says the citizens appear to be ex-military for the most part."

Hicks spoke up. "That elfish guy you were talking about—I overheard some of the protest coordinators mention him. They were saying that the time had come to 'make him a martyr.' I think that means they are planning to execute him, doesn't it? It might not be a good time for him to come back to the city."

"Maybe that's why they are getting weapons," Chandler said.

"Nope," Hicks looked scornful. "They don't need weapons for this elfish guy. He's just one guy. The group could just grab him and stomp him or hang him or cut him up." Hicks said with gusto, "You don't need weapons for one guy."

"No," Chandler said, "but they might need weapons if they were going to attack the institute. The walls are extremely thick because of the power drawn and generated by the equipment in the lab. And because of the presence of the portal, the army has placed guards inside the fence."

"Which is electrified," Colt added.

Hicks shook his head. "Me and a couple of the protesters went and looked at that fence. It's electrified all right, but the connections are outside one of the outbuildings in plain sight. A high-velocity round would blow it up, and they don't have an emergency backup."

"Hicks, did the protest coordinators discuss anyone else at the institute? Did they mention any other names?"

"Nope, at least not when I was listening. They seemed to have an extremely bad case of hate on the elfish guy is all."

Piet Lem stood up and shook Hicks' hand in dismissal. Colt saw a cash token change hands, and Hicks hustled off, very happy with the praise and the cash.

Piet Lem resumed his seat. "What happened in the protester camp?"

Colt delivered a brief resume of the events in the camp leading Piet Lem to give Chandler a hard look when his apparent connection to Irene Thorne and Pelham was revealed. When Colt mentioned the fusion pistol, he glanced over at Colt's backpack and whistled silently. Colt finished by saying, "I think when Ana calls, she needs to be told to stay right where she is, with or without Dr. Elvistine. And I think in the interim, it's time Chandler tells us what his role in this mess seems to be."

"I agree," Piet Lem said. "But while he's talking, let's have some food. I've been out and about and need some tea and rice." He pulled out a comm and spoke briefly about the meal. Colt wondered if he was ordering more than lunch.

Very quickly a slight, young girl appeared, carrying a heavy tray holding tea equipage and a bottled of cognac. She distributed everything quickly and efficiently, smiled at all the men and departed. Piet Lem poured them all cups of tea and sloshed a dollop of cognac in the cups.

"To the Conclave of Elders and the New Dispensation," he toasted with his teacup. Colt and Chandler both repeated the customary toast, and they all drank.

Then Chandler said, "The truth of the matter is this: My father is a member of the Consistory of Elders, which serves a supporting function to the Conclave. Most citizens have not heard of the consistory. It consists of functionaries who carry out the organizational activities and policies of the C.E. My father's responsibilities have nothing to do with information gathering for the C.E., other officials are responsible for that. But he and his fellow officials are interested in knowing what is going on throughout the planet. The C.E. pursues a need-to-know policy even with their own people so each group within the Conclave and the consistory has freelance operatives traveling around gathering intel. My sphere of interest is this general location including the city, the Subs, and the countryside."

Colt thought, *anyone who says 'the truth of the matter is so-and-so' is lying by definition*, but he said, "You're a spy."

"Yeah, I guess so," Chandler said, "But look at it this way, through me you have a direct line to the C.E."

"So is it true, what Irene said, that a faction of elders are planning to enlarge the portal or open another one?" Colt asked.

"Yep. They think the cautious approach is a waste

of time, and they are convinced that contact with *the other side*, where and whatever that is, can be beneficial to them. Having conquered one planet, they are bored. They want to conquer something else." He sloshed some more cognac into his cup and took a sip.

The young girl then reappeared with an even larger tray laden with dishes of rice and vegetables and warm spiced fruit.

The three men fell to enthusiastically. Colt thought about the last few days and how many meals he had missed. Ana was already dangerously thin, and he had often tried to get her to eat. Maybe when this was all over, he would make more of an effort, try to get her to live a little bit of a normal life. If this were ever over.

As they ate, they discussed the protesters and the possibility that someone had a covert purpose in funding the group. Chandler said that the C.E. and the consistory were very interested in the possible threat the group might pose, especially in view of the fact, which Piet Lem knew and Colt was unaware of, that similar groups were forming in other cities. The goals of the different groups were slightly different but were congruent with the main strand of thought, i.e., they were afraid of the ephemerists. Chandler reported that the two modes of thought were represented among the C.E. and the members of consistory, as well. His family were primarily ephemerists, believing that the world was illusory and thus susceptible to being affected by thought, hence the concerns about the time theory.

Chandler went on to say that the ephemerists in the C.E. often pointed to the original organizational charter of the C.E., which had postulated a world organized around the principles enunciated by the C.E. For centuries the principles had been developed verbally, and teaching was passed from mentor to protégé within the order until a few decades before the plague when a group of elders had held a conference in the mountains and reduced the principles to a mandate. Within a generation, the plague had started, and within two generations, the C.E. had taken control of the planet. This was a powerful argument for the ephemerists members of the C.E., and the counterargument that it was all a coincidence seemed weak and simplistic.

In Chandler's view there were two paths to an apocalypse: the expansion of the portal either by enlarging the aperture in the city or by opening a new portal elsewhere, and the publication, dissemination, and discussion of the proof that time could not exist. Either one would so destabilize the ground of illusion upon which life depended that it would end.

"This sounds exactly like the agenda of the protesters," Piet Lem said.

"It is, and the ephemerists among the C.E. would support the protesters views completely were it not for the fact that the genesis and funding of the protest group is unknown. All members of the C.E. are pragmatists. They cannot accept that a mass movement that exactly supports their beliefs has accidentally developed among the citizens. That's why many of us are trying to find out who is funding the group and why. Now that they are being armed, the need to find out has become more urgent."

"Chandler, what do you think is Irene Thorne's role in all this?" Colt asked.

"I wish I knew. I *think* she is just a kook. Her plan to discredit Elvistine is not a bad one if it would work. But, like any governing body, the C.E. are worried when a citizen starts taking on their role. They would have been more worried if she had inherited her father's money, but when they fought just before he died," Chandler paused, "mysteriously died, he wasn't sick, he had cut her out of the will. All she had was her mother's money, which was a lot, but not enough to fund a private army."

"That's really what you think is happening? Someone is creating a private army. But for what purpose?"

Chandler smiled, "That's the question, isn't it?"

They ate in silence for a while. Somewhere in the catacombs a party was happening and music filtered through the halls to Piet Lem's chamber.

It was a strangely peaceful interlude.

After the meal, they sat around finishing the bottle of cognac and discussing this and that. Piet explained the Osiran religion to them, and they agreed that it made a lot of sense. Chandler talked a little bit about growing up inside the Conclave of Elders, but it didn't sound a lot different from anyone else's childhood. Colt told Piet Lem that one of Beau's friends had been reporting on him to Irene, and Piet promised to make the kid's life miserable when he was identified.

They tried to decide whether Tillman's proof that the portal must be a sham could, based on the principles of the ephemerists, actually invalidate the portal. That proposal was why Chandler had become close to Tillman and his circle. Whether Tillman's thesis could affect an established fact, given the cosmological basis of the ephemerist position, was dissected. They then drunkenly discussed what constituted a fact.

Eventually Hicks wandered back from some teenage ramble, and Piet ordered him to stay awake and to call them immediately when Ana got in touch. He happily agreed, being, Colt thought, in awe of himself for helping Piet and receiving props from his hero.

Full of food and cognac, having bonded over drunken philosophical discussions, the three men turned in.

Sometime later, Hicks awakened Colt with the news that Ana and Beau had met Dr. Elvistine in a small villages called White Swan and were staying at a local inn. They had decided to remain there for a day or two because the professor had been hurt escaping from his crashed air car and needed bed rest. Secure in this knowledge, Colt went back to sleep.

20

Three hung-over men had tea and sweet buns the next morning and complained about their stomachs. Piet Lem gave Colt a comm he swore was secure, and Colt called Ana. He was beginning to think that fearing for himself and Ana was just paranoia and that Dr. Elvistine was the person who needed to worry. Certainly Irene and her assassin Pelham were after him. Colt was glad he had taken the fusion pistol, but Pelham and Irene would be just as deadly with conventional arms. Colt was not convinced that Irene wanted to disgrace Dr. Elvistine. He thought she would be just as happy to see him dead or disappeared—after she found a way to secure his brilliant sperm.

Ana seemed relaxed and happy to talk to him. For his part, he missed her and wanted to see her. They agreed that she would stay where she was, at a little inn called The Golden Crane. She said it was nice to be in the countryside. Elvistine was in bed, resting from a concussion and a bad cut on his forehead.

Colt hung up feeling good about Ana and optimistic. He planned to go to White Swan and talk Ana and Dr. Elvistine into staying there until they could figure out what was happening in the city. Piet Lem had assured him that his contacts among the authorities had found no indication that they had any interest in Colt or Ana. They were still mildly interested in Arlo, whose name remained on several watch lists, but it was so far down those lists that no one was likely to bother him unless he did something stupid or high profile or both.

A quick call to Sparrow revealed that Linnet had completely dropped out of sight and none of the kids in the house seemed to know where she was. Sparrow said he believed them; they had no reason to lie.

With universal travel passes produced by Chandler and armed with both conventional and unconventional arms, they headed north toward White Swan while the light was still good. Getting there should take about four hours with the air car at full speed.

They set the coordinates, and the car lifted to a traveling height of two feet. They would take turns keeping an eye on the indicators, but the car also had a voice of its own that would alert passengers to problems from oil leaks to bandits.

The countryside was pleasantly warm. The area they were traversing consisted of rolling hills with occasional copses of trees. The sparse population farmed and tried to raise various types of animals on the short grass. In the distance, they could see the shadows of higher hills. The little town they were heading toward was at the base of a large hill and was positioned where wild animals were reputed to wander freely. The air car delivered frequent warnings not to approach any large cats, but they did not see any of the indigenous panthers or mutated bobcats.

They reached White Swan without incident and dropped the air car in front of the inn, a group of free-standing huts clustered around a central patio. The kitchen abutted the patio, and they saw Ana and Beau sitting at a table out in the open. Ana immediately ran to Colt and hugged him hard. Her hair was blowing, and she looked fresh and rested. Piet Lem and Beau gave each other manly one-arm hugs, and Beau was introduced to Chandler.

Ana merely gave Chandler a cool hello, and Colt remembered that she had not cared for him in the old days.

Dr. Elvistine was eating from a tray in one of the cabins when Colt stuck his head in to say hello. The prof looked wan and unfocused, picking at his food.

When he went back to the group, who had pulled over a bigger table and were giving the waiter orders, he told them that he was unhappy with Elvistine's appearance. To Colt, his head injury looked very severe, and he wanted to know what local clinic had examined him. Ana said they had not taken the doctor to a clinic. He had not wanted to go, and Beau had cleaned and bandaged his head wound.

Neither of them had checked out the pupils of his eyes or done any of the tests to identify a severe concussion. Colt wished he had one of the doctors from his cage-fighting days to take a look. They could practically smell severe head trauma.

Piet Lem went to the office and made arrangements for the three men to share a cabin—

there were plenty of vacancies—and determined that the nearest decent sized clinic was two hours by air car in a large shore town called Deep Cove.

Ana said, "Teegan and Jordi are in Deep Cove. Our roommates and old friends," she added for Piet Lem and Chandler's benefit. "They freaked out because they were being followed and went there to stay with friends."

Colt had a lot to tell Ana, but he wanted to talk with Elvistine first, to try to get a better feel for his condition.

But when they returned to Dr. Elvistine's room, his condition had deteriorated. He appeared to be unconscious, and they determined that he must be transferred to the clinic immediately. Piet Lem offered to contact the clinic for a helicopter, but they decided that it would probably take as long to get a helicopter as it would to take the air car, especially since the land between White Swan and Deep Cove was a kind of scrubby desert sloping downward to the sea, easily traveled by the air car, which could leave immediately.

Ana and Colt would travel in the air car with the professor while Piet Lem, Beau, and Chandler would follow later. They easily transferred Elvistine's slight frame from the cabin to the car.

After Colt and Ana left with the professor, Chandler contacted the clinic to alert them of the air car's expected arrival. The innkeeper had said that the route between White Swan and Deep Cove was safe; the land too sparsely traveled to attract bandits. Tourists would approach the seaside town via the train which ran along the coast by sea. White Swan's attraction for tourists was the hunting in the nearby hills now that the wildlife had begun to return.

One of the villagers, a dark, runty citizen named Kalib, ran a for-hire transport business using a rugged hybrid vehicle that could double as an air car and wheeled vehicle for uneven terrain. He was willing to drive the three men to Deep Cove for a price and was willing to leave immediately despite the impending darkness. He had good lights on the hybrid, he said, and patting a hatch in the door, a fusion grenade launcher if problems arose. He would stay the night in Deep Cove.

Piet Lem offered to make the innkeeper whole for the rooms they had not used, but he refunded their deposits without comment. Ana had paid in advance for her room, so they were square, he said. The innkeeper, an elderly, experienced citizen, was happy to see them go, sensing that they might be involved in activities that would attract the attention of the authorities or, worse, in the countryside, the C.E. militia.

He saw them off with a cheerful, much-relieved wave.

During the trip, Colt used the air car's communication device to contact Teegan and Jordi in Deep Cove, where they were staying with old friends, Rick and Ilsa, from the university. Teegan answered the comm, sounding none too happy to hear from Colt, and when she understood the situation, she became even more tense. Nevertheless, she said she would make arrangements for Colt and Ana to stay in a guest house next to Rick's cottage. As she parted, she said, "You know the protesters have declared a bounty on Dr. Elvistine, so you better be careful."

Ending the conversation, Colt relayed the information to Ana, who was understandably upset. They decided the simplest story would be to tell the clinic staff that the patient's name was Abram Bede, Ana's father's name, and that all his ID had been lost in the air car ambush. They could check that Abram Bede showed up in various data bases; Elvistine was the right age; and Ana and Colt had ID showing that their last name was the same as the injured man.

The clinic was on the edge of the small town, set off from the track. It included a cluster of small white buildings and a heliport. By the presence of the heliport, Colt judged that the clinic provided services for a large area. Once the whine of the air car system was silenced, Colt, a city boy, was struck by the silence of the countryside. In his military career, he had only been in the countryside for the mandatory training exercises. Because he was a military athlete, he was stationed in various cities where matches were held. The silence of the countryside made him feel as is his head was going to implode.

He had stopped the air car by the emergency entrance and attendants immediately ran out with stretchers and other equipment. The attendant in charge took their particulars and glanced indifferently at Colt and Ana's ID. Ana explained how her father's papers had been lost in the ambush, an explanation which the attendant accepted without interest. The patient was hustled into the building and surrounded immediately by competent-looking pastel-clad medical personnel. The sounds they made were not encouraging.

They settled down in a waiting room but Colt was

incapable of sitting still for too long and left Ana doodling formulae on a note pad. He walked outside into the salty smelling air and got the air car comm unit from the vehicle which was parked around back of the clinic. Colt felt unhappy and exposed in the flat, empty landscape, like a target, expecting a laser bullet to come out of nowhere to take him down.

Teegan again answered the comm. "Teegan, it's me, Colt. Don't Rick and Ilsa ever answer their own comm?"

"They are at a fair in town today. Jordi went with them, but I stayed here to do some drawing." There was something in her voice that told Colt she was lying, but he was too involved with his own problems to care. Teegan was a compulsive liar.

"Just wanted to let you know that Ana is with *her father, Abram Bede*, at the clinic. *Her father* is not doing well. He is unconscious, and the medical people think he is badly hurt." He stressed the message, hoping she would pick up on his intention.

"This is just too bad. Ana and *her father* are so close." She said, mimicking his tone. "But you are set for the guest house. Rick's guests use it all the time, and it's very comfortable."

Colt wanted to know if there would be room for three other guests when they arrived, and Teegan, none to happy to begin with, was even less happy when she heard who the guests were.

"The only thing that would make this worse is if you-know-who were here," she said. Colt inferred that she meant Arlo, and he realized he had briefly forgotten all about Arlo.

"We'll talk more when we see you. Ana will want to stay at the clinic, but she'll need some food and sleep at some point. We'll call for directions before we come over."

"I'm not happy about this," she said as she terminated the conversation.

21

When Colt returned to the waiting room, Ana was in conversation with an authoritative figure in a long white robe wearing the icon of a healer. The icon included the sign for a scalpel indicating that he was authorized to operate. No one used scalpels any more. Lasers had replaced such antiquated and clumsy equipment years before, but the scalpels endured as the symbol of the surgeon.

"This citizen is the chief surgeon, Healer Bruxton," Ana said. "He has bad news." Ana brushed a tear from her face.

The healer had a pretentious, rumbling delivery that set Colt's teeth on edge. He flipped amber worry beads endlessly and avoided their eyes. "I'm sorry to say there was a lot of bleeding into the brain and the long delay in getting medical attention made matters worse." His irritation seemed personal.

"Did my wife explain to you that her father was attacked by bandits and just managed to escape"

The citizen jiggled his beads. "I'm impressed that a man his age and with his heart condition could have pulled that off. One would have thought his heart would give out on him with that kind of exertion. But it is just the exertion that made the bleeding into the brain worse. Had he gotten immediate attention, we could have stabilized the condition. At this point, there is little we can do, I'm afraid. We have stopped the bleeding, but the damage is done."

Colt took Ana in his arms to comfort her.

"What do you mean about his heart condition? We . . . we didn't know he had a heart condition." She spoke through tears.

"I'm sure he was trying to keep you from worrying, but he had a serious heart condition that could have been fatal at any moment. The onset of a fatal attack could have been triggered by anything, even something very minor. I'm surprised the bandit attack didn't do it. Even overwork or exhaustion could have led to a terminal event."

The surgeon fiddled with a thick gold chain on his wrist; its color complemented the amber beads. Apparently surgeons were quite prosperous, Colt thought.

"He believed that mental exhaustion could enhance the creative faculties," Ana said.

"In that case, I'm surprised he didn't succumb long ago. This condition is congenital and present even in young people. It becomes more dangerous with age, of course. Do you have brothers, Ms. Bede?"

Ana looked surprised at the question, forgetting the fiction that the patient was her father. Colt answered for her. "No, Ana has no brothers. That's why I took her name when we married."

"Good. Because the condition favors the male children. Occasionally a female will inherit, but it is rare." The surgeon was restless and ready to move on. He turned to leave.

"I have one question, citizen," Colt said. "Can this condition be cured by prenatal DNA manipulation like other chronic conditions that have been eliminated?"

"No. A handful of conditions do not lend themselves to PDM. This is one of them."

"So the patient would not have made a good sperm donor?"

The physician looked appalled. "Absolutely not. No reputable reproductive facility would accept sperm from such a donor." He looked sharply at Ana. "I expect you were conceived in situ," he said.

"Oh, yes," she stuttered. "I must have been. We never discussed it."

"Well, you should have." He held out a fist to Colt to bump. "But I must go. I have other patients. We'll do all we can for your father, but I'm afraid he will not last the night. I'll arrange for you to sit with him if you want to."

"Thank you. I'll do that." Ana said.

He stalked away, glancing purposefully at the hospital comm attached to his wrist.

Colt walked with Ana back to the professor's room. He was plugged into a machine that recorded a gentle, irregular heartbeat, and his head had been professionally bandaged. His eyes were closed, and he appeared at rest.

Ana sat down next to him and took his hand.

Colt went down the hall to an attendant's station

to make sure Ana would have some tea. He knew she would not eat when she was this upset, but getting some tea into her would help. The attendant, a motherly looking eunuch of the type that seems to gravitate to the medical field, assured him she would have tea. "We'll slip some energy drops in her tea. They will give her a boost and provide some microscopic cell nourishment. They are designed for this type of situation."

Colt was grateful. "I'm going to our guest house for a while. Please make sure she contacts me if something happens before I return."

The attendant assured him it would be done.

Colt called Rick's house and talked with Teegan once more, obtaining the location of the guesthouse. Piet Lem and the others had already arrived. It was close to the clinic so Colt jogged along the path toward the villages. Rick and Ilsa's cottage was typical of others in the area: a large square building with a flat top accessible by an external staircase. An open archway led to an interior court. Colt rang the bell which hung from a wood support, and Rick emerged from the back of the house. Colt had taken classes from him at university and wondered if he would be remembered. He wasn't.

"You must be Colt." They fist-bumped and Rick quickly turned and walked toward the rear of the building. "The others are out back." He didn't seem particularly happy and, under the circumstances, Colt could not blame him.

Jordi and Rick's wife, Ilsa, sat at a table on the terrace. Piet, Beau, and Chandler sat like kids on the low, wide wall that surrounded two sides of the terrace. Rick joined Jordi and Ilsa at the table and nodded curtly toward a fourth chair. Colt had never seen Ilsa. The love affair between the two had been notorious, and Rick had chosen to resign from the university to avoid trouble.

Rick had been sixty and Ilsa eighteen when they met. Members of the faculty suspected that Rick had motivations other than infatuation with the beautiful and talented young woman. It was generally known that she had been tested and found fertile. It could be a gold mine for Rick or anyone who acted as her agent. Rick, however, had loudly refused to let her become a surrogate, infuriating those who were having to wait years and pay huge amounts of cash for services.

Rick had been a handsome, vigorous sixty and was now a handsome vigorous seventy. Living in the more liberal atmosphere of the shore, he had let his iron-grey hair grow into a long braid similar to that sported by Chandler, but without the fighting ball. Ilsa had been and still was an extraordinary beauty. She sat with her back to the sea, slender and regal, her dark hair swept back from her forehead held in place by a beaded band of unusual style and intricacy. Her large, azure eyes slanted slightly upward. To see her was to be mesmerized by her beauty which was enhanced by a deep, compelling voice. She had been trained as a singer, but Rick had refused to let her perform because it would require her to travel extensively. Despite the limitations of living in a small seaside town with a man forty-two years older than she, Ilsa looked happy and content. She greeted Colt in a friendly way and rose to pour him a glass of wine.

Despite Ilsa's easy hospitality, an atmosphere of

constraint colored the group. Rick was grumpy, and Colt, who knew Jordi well, could see that, behind his usual unruffled demeanor, he was upset. Piet Lem and Chandler were chatting amiably while Beau was frankly smitten with Ilsa, showing off and trying to engage her in conversation.

Colt filled them in on Elvistine's condition. Teegan had told Rick and Ilsa about the bounty on Elvistine and warned them to say nothing about the real identity of the man in the clinic. Ilsa was concerned about Ana's real father; when Elvistine died using his name, the clinic would report his passing. Chandler was frankly pleased at the turn events had taken. Colt also was relieved. he had no personal feelings one way or the other about the professor but with Elvistine out of the way, Ana could justifiably claim her ability to enlarge or open a portal depended on him. As far as the proof of the non-existence of time, Colt did not share Chandler's concern with it and was unsure about Ana's ability or interest in continuing the work on her own.

Colt could see that Rick was extremely angry at having his quiet sanctuary invaded by people from the city. Colt was not sure he blamed him. Entertaining in one's home was not something people did.

The only citizen not in evidence was Teegan. Colt preferred to know where everyone was when the atmosphere was as troubled as this one. He found her on a little terrace at the front of the house, one that had a view of the hills in the distance. She was sketching and drinking vodka. The terrace was surrounded by a waist-high wall, and lizards chased each other across the top. A cat lay in one corner, in the sun, its eyes shielded by its tail.

Colt was taken aback by the cat, which could be a plague carrier. Teegan saw him looking at it and laughed. "The cat's okay. It's been tested. Besides everyone knows the plague was not spread by cats. It came from the sky. Probably from the airships of the Conclave of Elders."

Colt was shocked at her assertion, even though he had heard it before, especially from Arlo.

"Arlo used to say things like that," he said.

"He still does." She gave Colt a look he could not quite analyze, then went back to sketching. "Rick is furious at you for bringing all these people to Deep Cove. He's afraid one of them will steal Ilsa from him. He's not getting any younger."

"Maybe Ilsa doesn't want to get stolen." Colt dropped to the ground and crossed his legs gracefully.

"All women can be stolen if the price is tempting enough." She continued sketching and smiling to herself.

"And what's Ilsa's price?"

"I think she would be angry at giving up singing. She trained for it from a child, but Rick was afraid to let her perform in public because someone with more money or prestige would lure her away. But she's not likely to run into such a person here in Deep Cove."

"Did you know Chandler in college?" Colt changed the subject.

"Yes, I knew him quite well." She put her sketch book down and poured herself another drink.

"Did you know he had family connections in the Conclave?"

"You mean the consistory? I know that's what he said. I never saw him do anything to prove it, but it could be true. It didn't matter anyway because he was a serious guy who spent most of his time studying. He was Tillman's protégé."

"As was Arlo?" Making it a question.

"Arlo was Tillman's protégé, but not in mathematics or theoretical physics."

Colt flowed upward and was on his feet, walking toward the wall. The cat switched its tail and glared at him.

"I get it. Tillman was the one who got Arlo involved with the terrorist group."

"Yes. Tillman was behind it all. He still is, wherever he is."

"Arlo knows where he is," Colt said.

Teegan just said "yes" and sipped her drink.

Things were coming together in Colt's mind. "Arlo is not in love with Ana any longer, is he?"

She smiled smugly when she said, "No."

"He's in love with you."

"Yes."

"Are you going to leave Jordi?"

"Yes."

"Does he know it?

"He doesn't believe it. He thinks I'll change my mind."

Colt gazed at the horizon. The landscape here was entirely too empty, he thought. Jordi was like his brother. He would be devastated if Teegan left him for Arlo. Especially Arlo.

"I don't get it," Colt said over his shoulder. "Jordi is a beautiful guy, handsome, kind, fun, and he is devoted to you. Arlo is none of these things, and he's unsanctioned, He can't work anywhere or travel freely. And you think you are in love with him."

Behind him, Teegan said, "Jordi is a sweet guy, and

I hate to hurt him. But Arlo has things Jordi doesn't have. He has a mission, he has convictions."

Colt turned around to stare at her for this crazy talk. She held up the picture she had been sketching. It showed a drawing of a terrace much like the one they were using at the moment, but with domes and gardens in the distance, similar to illustrations in the books they read as children. In Teegan's picture, she had drawn a bolt of lighting striking the center of the terrace and the elders in their long white robes were lying dead.

"Oh, Teegan," he said. "Don't let anyone see that."

She laughed, and he realized just how little he knew about her.

Colt leaned on the wall and looked with unseeing eyes toward the road. Suddenly and with jarring intensity, a loud noise erupted in the sky and a helicopter came into view, over the water, landing on a flat section of road in front of the villa.

The rotors slowed, and four people got out of the machine, leaving the pilot behind. Irene Thorne and Pelham were both armed, Irene with a shotgun and Pelham with a conventional pistol. Linnet and a man Colt didn't recognize were unarmed. All four ran into the building. Colt had left his backpack with the fusion pistol downstairs in the foyer, but he had his small pistol and a knife in his pants. Below him the sound of screaming and a pistol shot sounded. Colt ran softly downstairs and through several rooms to the balcony where Piet Lem, Rick, Chandler, Beau, and Ilsa stood with their backs against the waist-high wall, their hands in the air. Jordi was on the floor with blood flowing from his chest. Teegan rushed past

Colt and knelt next to him, trying to stop the blood with her hands. Linnet, in tears, and the unknown man were seated at a table with their hands flat on the top in front of them. Colt stopped in the shadows of a doorway almost directly across from Irene. Pelham stood to her left near Chandler. Irene was saying, "This shotgun is set on fan, so if anyone moves, I can shoot at least three of you and Pel here will shoot the rest, so just be quiet."

Piet Lem and Chandler were standing calmly with Beau, who looked scared, his head down, sweating. He's just a kid. Colt thought of himself at that age, he would be terrified.

Rick, leaning hard against the wall and looking scores older than he had just half an hour before, quavered out a question; when he was ignored by Irene and Pelham, he put a hand to his chest. Ilsa flinched and said, "He has a bad heart. Let me get his medicine." She made a gesture as if to move.

"No," Irene screamed. "Don't move." She's hysterical, Colt thought, and the shotgun is probably on a hair trigger. He hoped she wouldn't notice him lurking in the doorway. "Where's Elvistine?" she screamed again. "I know you have him. I know he was in White Swan. We had a tracker in his shoe. He left his shoes in that crummy inn. He must be here somewhere. I have to find him."

Chandler said conversationally, "How did you find us here, Irene?"

"You want to know if I'm tracking you, don't you, you unsanctioned bastard?"

"I do, Irene," he said softly.

"I don't need to. Beau here sent a message to his girlfriend in the Subs, and she was able to track it back."

Beau jerked his head up. "Rowan told you?" He sounded close to tears. "Dad. . ." he appealed then choked up.

Piet Lem just shook his head.

"What is it you want exactly, Irene?" Chandler asked.

"Elvistine. I'm going to take him to the nearest fertility center, and he is going to give me his sperm, and then I'm going to kill him. Pelham here can collect the bounty."

"You want him to impregnate you?" Ilsa sounded incredulous.

"Not me, you stupid woman. Her." She waved the shotgun at Linnet, who flinched. "I had her tested. She's fertile. She can carry a child or, with luck, twins or triplets, to term."

"Then you are going to kill her?" Chandler said.

Irene was surprised at the question. She gave it some thought. "I don't know. that's a question for another day."

The stranger next to Linnet started to lunge upward, but Linnet grabbed his arm. He was not from the city, Colt realized. His clothes were utilitarian, heavy and rugged, and his hands on the table were work-hardened. This must be the husband, Colt thought, from the community—Heartsease. He must have come to the city to get his wife.

"Shall I shoot him?" Pelham asked Irene.

"No. I promised Linnet that I would let him live if she cooperated with me." Irene's face started to change, like she was going to cry. She turned to Linnet and spoke in a soft crooning voice. "Linnet, baby, Linnet. I love you. You know that. From the moment I saw you in that horrible sex club, I knew I would love you. Why can't you love me? We could have my beautiful, brilliant babies. They would be the new rulers. The protesters are almost ready to begin the resistance. The materialist faction in the Conclave of Elders are ready to act. We could be the queens of the new world. You don't need this, this, this farmer."

As she spoke, she had moved closer to Linnet and pointed her shotgun away from Piet Lem and Chandler. Pelham, a little behind her and to her left, looked away from Chandler and Piet Lem briefly, a look of contempt on his face.

Chandler made a sudden, incredibly quick move of his head, faster than an eye could follow, and the fighting ball struck the back of Pelham's skull, crushing it and killing him instantly.

Colt, seeing his moment, threw his knife at Irene's wrist, severing the tendons. When the shotgun dropped it discharged, scattering shot that missed everyone but Colt, a few shot penetrating his pant leg and burying into his shin.

Piet Lem stepped behind Irene and chopped down on the back of her neck, dropping her to the ground.

Chaos erupted as Ilsa ran to Rick and Teegan screamed for them to get help for Jordi. Amid the noise, Ana stepped onto the terrace, in tears.

They all looked at her, and there was a moment of silence caused by her look of intense grief. She spread her hands from her side, hands facing upward, like a child, and said, "Dr. Elvistine has gone. He left a few minutes ago."

"He's dead," someone said, with finality.

"No. No," Ana said. "He activated a portal. Dr. Elvistine has left the world."

Ana began bawling. Colt moved to comfort her, holding her and talking softly. She pushed him away, angry. "You don't understand," she said. "This is terrible. This could mean the end everything. I told you, Colt.

"Armageddon."

ABOUT THE AUTHOR

A career bureaucrat, Rachel Winters retired to Central Florida where she lives with her husband and two Chihuahuas. When not writing deeply existential science fiction, she plays Mah Jongg and plans trips to remote spots around the world.